T
'Why don't you sleep your way into pictures . . . what's your name?'

'Jason . . .'

'Jason?'

'Because I don't have the tits.' He thought it was funny. But Hanna wasn't laughing. She was unzipping her skirt.

'Fuck me.'

'What?'

'You heard. I want you to fuck me. It'll do your career no end of good.'

'And if I don't?'

'Goodbye career.' Now she was laughing. She stripped off her skirt revealing lacy white French knickers.

'And if I do?'

'That depends, doesn't it? Come on, I've had a hard day. Come over here and rake the grass off my lawn.'

'Do I get the part?'

'You learn fast, Jason.'

# The Casting Couch

Becky Bell

**Delta**

First published in 1994
by HEADLINE BOOK PUBLISHING

A HEADLINE DELTA paperback

10 9 8 7 6 5 4 3 2

ISBN 0 7472 4453 7

Typeset by Avon Dataset Ltd., Bidford-on-Avon

Printed and bound in Great Britain by
Mackays of Chatham plc, Chatham, Kent

HEADLINE BOOK PUBLISHING
A division of the Hodder Headline Group
338 Euston Road,
London NW1 3BH

www.headline.co.uk
www.hodderheadline.com

# The Casting Couch

# Chapter One

Jason MacIver was an actor. It was official now, after three years at RADA. He was a good actor. That was official too, after he had won the gold medal for the best student in his final year. He was also out of work. It had been five months since all the excitement of winning the award and having his picture in the *Evening Standard* hugging Molly Hanson who had won the female prize. But he wasn't worried. The prize had meant he had been taken on by one of the top agents in London and he had already had five auditions and the promise of work with the RSC in the spring of next year if only as a spear-carrier. Jason had an optimistic personality, always looking on the bright side of life. He *knew* his break would come and come quickly.

Jason had no money. He was permanently broke. But that didn't worry him either. He would be rich one day, when he got his break. Meantime he worked part time in whatever job he could get – burger joints, delivering pizzas, hod-carrying – to pay the bills.

He took his chosen profession seriously. He continued to go to voice and singing classes, he made sure he went to as many plays as possible to watch and learn from other actors and he kept his body in shape with regular games of tennis, long hours of fencing instruction and daily visits to a gym. The gym he frequented was not a fashionable club packed with high-tech exercise machines designed to take the sweat out of training, but an unfashionable low-tech boxer's gym in the Mile End Road. There he could work out on the hard bag, use weights, medicine balls and wall bars, honing his body to fitness. In fact, stripped down, his body looked very much like a boxer's: hard contoured arms, a deep chest and a flat iron stomach deeply lined with the definition of his 'apts'. Each rib was visible like the rungs of a ladder and his legs were muscular and strong. There was no doubt that Jason MacIver was in very good condition.

Nature had been on his side too. Jason was tall, six-foot-two in his stockinged feet, with hair so blond many women would have envied it, and piercing blue eyes, a deep turquoise blue. He was a person who was capable of being very still; he did not fidget when sitting or shift his weight from one foot to the other when standing and this had the effect, combined with those steely blue eyes, of disconcerting people, especially women. Jason was not a man who had ever had any trouble with his sex life.

He was working on the hard bag, hammering it with left and right combinations at waist level, sweat pouring into his track suit, his hands bound in boxer's tape, when the call came. It was his agent, or rather his agent's assistant.

'Have you got a pen?' she asked. Of course he hadn't.

'What is it?'

'It's a film. A big one. American money. Major studio picture. American director. Half made here, half in LA. They want a newcomer for the young lead. The producer is here at

2

the moment. We've sent them your pics and they're interested.'

'Great!' Jason could feel his heart thumping and not from the exercise.

'You've got to go to the Dorchester. Four-thirty tomorrow. Have you written that down?'

She must be mad. Did she seriously think he'd forget it?

'You're meeting Hanna Silverstein, she's the producer, and George Mason.'

'*The* George Mason?'

'That's him. Good, isn't it?'

'Great! Fantastic! How did you manage it?'

'They say to go looking casual. Don't wear a suit.'

'The lead?'

'The lead. Go get it, Jason.'

'Listen, that's really great. Thank Joy for me, will you?'

'Oh, Joy says Hanna Silverstein is a real ball-breaker so not to worry if she's rude. It's just her way, apparently.'

Joy Chivas was his agent. She spoke to him rarely. In fact, she'd only spoken to him once since they'd had their first meeting. If he got this film she would, no doubt, be on the phone in person.

'I'll be there.'

'Good luck.'

'Thanks. Thanks a lot. Will they give me a script to read, by the way?'

'Don't know . . .'

Well, he thought, as he put the phone down and went back into the gym to hammer the hard bag with renewed enthusiasm, this might well be just the break he knew, in his heart of hearts, that he was sure to get.

It took Jason a long time to decide what he was going to wear but, in the end, having posed in the mirror in six or seven combinations, he decided on jeans, a crisp white shirt and his one expensive jacket – a leather Armani he had worked overtime in a pub for three consecutive weekends to afford.

He took a taxi. It was an extravagance but psychologically it made him feel better, more important and substantial. Besides, he didn't want to arrive with his carefully brushed hair rearranged by gusts of wind as he walked down the street or got on the tube.

The commissionaire, smartly uniformed with a gold-braided cap, open the door of the taxi as soon as it came to rest.

'Good afternoon, sir,' he said, saluting.

'Good afternoon,' Jason replied, hoping he did not expect a tip. Apparently, as he continued to smile when Jason walked passed him into the hotel, he didn't.

Breezing into the main lobby with its marble floors, decorative gilt plaster work and fine oriental carpeting, Jason made for the reception desk.

'Hanna Silverstein, please,' he said politely.

'Who may I say it is, sir?' the immaculately suited man behind the desk asked, his morning coat and pin-striped trousers looking as though they had just come straight from the hotel laundry.

'Jason MacIver.'

'Thank you, Mr MacIver.'

In ten minutes Jason was standing outside the door of the Oliver Messel Suite on the top floor. He knocked tentatively and the door was opened, after a moment, by a smartly dressed, tall and incredibly attractive brunette who Jason guessed to be in her mid-twenties.

'Ms Silverstein?' he said, stressing the Ms.

'No, I'm Camilla Potts,' she said in a soft American accent. 'Come in. You're Jason MacIver, right? Very prompt. You're the last appointment of the day. Follow me.'

Jason was surprised to find a flight of stairs inside the door. Camilla lead the way. It was not an uninteresting prospect as her slender ankles and nylon-clad legs mounted the stairs in front of him. He could never remember seeing a more shapely pair of legs and, since the skirt of her suit was short, there was a lot of them to see.

'Are you Ms Silverstein's assistant? Jason asked trying to make conversation.

'Hell no. Just a friend of the family helping out for the day.'

At the top of the stairs the panorama of London unfolded in front of him. A wall of windows revealed a view of Buckingham Palace on one side and Hyde Park Corner on the other. No wonder, he thought, that these suites cost so much. Camilla showed him into the library, at least it was a room lined with books. On closer examination most of the books were fakes, their spines mocked-up in cardboard.

'She won't be long I'm sure,' Camilla said, closing the door behind her and leaving him to contemplate the view.

Almost immediately the door opened again. It took him a moment to recognise the man who entered. It was George Mason. He was a lot shorter than Jason would have imagined and had put on a lot of weight since his last published photograph. He was also very drunk.

'Is this the fucking bathroom?' he drawled.

'No,' Jason said, not at all sure what to say or do.

'Where is it?'

'I don't know.'

'What the fuck *do* you know?'

'I'm here to see Hanna Silverstein and you, sir.'

'Where's the bathroom then? I've got to take a leak.' He slumped into one of the armchairs unable to stand up any longer.

'Shall I go and find it?'

'Yes, make yourself useful.'

Jason walked out into the suite again. There was no sign of Camilla or anyone else. He tried a couple of doors after knocking and getting no reply. Behind both were bedrooms. He had found his way into the dining-room of the suite before he realised that in such a grand hotel each bedroom would be sure to have its own bathroom.

He walked back to the first bedroom be had found and went in. It appeared to be unoccupied. There were three identical doors on one wall. The first he tried was a wardrobe quite empty of clothes. The second, as he'd guessed, was a bathroom. Unfortunately this was not empty. In the middle of the white marble tiling Camilla Potts stood absolutely naked. In fact that was not quite true. She was wearing the black high heels Jason had followed up the stairs. As the bathroom was mirrored on every wall there was no part of Camilla that was not available for Jason's inspection, but she did not seem to be in the least concerned.

'Yes?' she said as coolly as if she were sitting behind a reception desk. She turned round to face him. Her breasts were extraordinary; though as full and rounded as any Jason had seen, they seemed to defy gravity, the nipples pointing upwards.

Her movement had produced a ripple in their flesh and they bounced and quivered at him. But even more noticeable was that Camilla's pubis was completely hairless. Whether natural or shaved he didn't know, but, as she stood now with legs akimbo, there was not a detail of her labia, her clitoris, the whole slit of her sex, that he could not see.

'Yes?' she repeated.

'George Mason. He can't find the bathroom,' he blurted out.

'Well, that's nothing new. You'll gather he has a drink problem?'

'Yes,' he said, trying desperately to pull his eyes from her naked body to her face. 'He doesn't look very well.'

'That's putting it mildly.'

She had picked up a pair of black French knickers from a neat pile of clothes on the bathroom stool and stepped into them. They slid over her long thighs to fit perfectly over the strong curve of her arse, the action reflected from every angle by the mirrors in the bathroom.

'Shall I bring him in here . . . I mean . . .'

'I'll come and get him.'

She was slipping into a black strapless bra, lifting the cups over her large breasts, clipping the fastening behind her back, then pulling each cup in turn to settle the breasts more comfortably in their lacy restraints.

Jason didn't know whether to go or stay now his mission was accomplished. He decided to go.

'Hold on,' she said.

She had stepped into a black silk evening dress, cut to mid-thigh and supported only by the thinnest of spaghetti straps which hooked over her shoulders. The dress revealed, as it was no doubt intended to do, a deep dark tunnel of cleavage.

'Zip me up, could you?'

Jason obliged with shaking hands.

'Thanks,' she said kissing his cheek with the briefest touch of her lips.

She escorted him out of the bathroom, back to the library, as naturally as if he'd just stepped out of her office. George Mason had vanished.

The phone rang. Camilla answered it.

'You're on. Good luck.'

She showed him a door at the end of the long corridor. 'What about Mr Mason?'

'He won't have gone far. I've got to go.' She looked at her watch. It was a Cartier. 'Thanks for the help.'

'My pleasure,' he mumbled, meaning it.

As he walked down the corridor and saw Camilla leaving the suite, the vision of her naked body haunted him. Her pouting labia, pink and smooth, nestling at the top of those long legs. Let alone her breasts, heavy but upturned. He couldn't get it out of his mind, and he was supposed to be concentrating on getting himself a very important job.

'Come!' a thick accent from the American south shouted in reply to his knock on the door.

He entered another bedroom. This one was arranged with a large desk facing the door. The desk was covered with papers, scripts and photographs. He could see his own ten-by-eight lying in a pile with a lot of others. Behind the desk Hanna Silverstein sat smoking a long brown cigarette. She was not what he had expected. She was blonde, natural as far as he could tell, and wearing a white suit decorated with large gold buttons. Her face was tanned, rather over-tanned, but though she must have been over fifty-five her face had remarkably few lines and wrinkles. She was not tall but her body was well-proportioned and neat with not an ounce of fat.

An empty bottle of champagne stood on the desk together with an empty glass.

'Your name?' she asked, not smiling, lifting her glasses to read from a piece of paper on the desk. From the way she slurred her words she was quite clearly drunk.

'Jason MacIver.'

'That's right. Have we met before?'

'No.'

'Oh.' She took her glasses off and got up. 'Look, it's been a long day for me. Perhaps we could do this in the morning.'

'Sure,' Jason said, trying to keep the disappointment out of his voice.

Hanna picked up the phone and punched in one number. Somewhere in the suite Jason could hear a phone ringing. No one answered it.

'If you want Ms Potts I think she went out.'

'Out where?'

'George Mason's missing.'

'He's not missing. He'll be downstairs in the bar.'

There was an awkward pause. Jason didn't know whether he had been dismissed.

'Do me a favour. Get me another bottle of champagne from the kitchen and open it. I'm hopeless with corks.'

It took Jason five minutes to find the kitchen, and the champagne. Hanna Silverstein drunk the first glass he poured for her quickly and held out the empty glass for a refill immediately.

'Join me, I hate drinking alone,' she said, indicating a glass on a side table.

The bottle disappeared rapidly despite the fact that Jason had only sipped at his glass. He was dispatched to get another. This time, when he returned, Hanna was lying on the bed. He poured the wine into her glass on the bedside table.

'So why don't you sleep your way into pictures . . . what's your name?'

'Jason . . .'

'Jason?'

'Because I don't have the tits.' He thought it was funny. But Hanna wasn't laughing. She was unzipping her skirt.

'Fuck me.'

'What?'

'You heard. I want you to fuck me. It'll do your career no end of good.'

'And if I don't?'

'Goodbye career.' Now she was laughing. She stripped off her skirt revealing lacy white French knickers.

'And if I do.'

'That depends, doesn't it? Come on, I've had a hard day. Come over here and rake the grass off my lawn.'

'Do I get the part?'

'You learn fast, Jason.'

She caught him by the hand and with surprising strength pulled him on top of her. Immediately her mouth clamped on to his and her hot tongue was forcing its way between his lips. Her hands were all over him, pulling his shirt out of his trousers, unzipping his jeans, squeezing his tight buttocks, feeling for his cock.

His mind was racing. The woman was drunk. She might regret it in the morning and then he'd have no chance. On the other hand, she might know exactly what she was doing, and if he refused he would have no chance either. His agent had said Hanna was a ball-breaker but he'd had no idea she meant literally.

His body made the decision for him. Hanna had shucked her way out of her jacket and blouse and now in white bra and French knickers, was burrowing her head down into Jason's lap. Her fingers had pulled his pants down far enough to reveal his cock and Hanna's mouth fixed on it like a limpet on a rock, impossible to remove. As she sucked and licked and tongued his cock he felt his erection swelling in her mouth. As soon as it was hard she came up for air.

'Good boy,' she said, pulling off her knickers. 'Now give it to me.' She lay back, her hand still wrapped around his cock, not bothering to take off her bra. He was committed now. It was too late to walk away. So if he was going to fuck her he might as well make a good job of it, he thought.

Jason rolled over on to his side and pulled himself down the bed, kissing Hanna's flesh as he went. When his mouth reached her hips he moved over her, kissing and licking his way over her navel until be reached the wispy blonde pubic hair. She opened her legs wider. His tongue found her clitoris. He had always loved cunnilingus and all his lovers had said he was good at it. Well, if this was the casting couch he was going to make sure Hanna didn't forget him in the morning. He started playing with her clitoris, circling it with his tongue, tapping it, nudging it, then running his tongue down to dart into the moist passage of her cunt. Within seconds be could feel her juices on his tongue, within minutes Hanna was shaking with orgasm, a long series of moans escaping from her lips.

'Well, you are a find,' she said, pulling his head up from her cunt. 'Now I want cock.'

He climbed up over her holding his cock at the entrance to her cunt, feeling her fleshy labia against his glans.

'You want it?' he asked, looking into this stranger's eyes, now quite wild with lust.

'Yes, yes, yes,' she screamed.

'Take it then,' he said as he pushed his cock home, sinking it to the hilt in one long, hard stroke. Immediately he was deep inside her Hanna bucked her hips up at him pushing his cock in and out, reinforcing his own strokes, controlling the rhythm. She wanted it hard and deep and frequent. The rhythm she established was frantic, like riding a horse in the rodeo, but he managed to stay in the saddle and give as good as he got. She bucked and kicked and scratched. She bit his shoulder and scored his back with her nails but he stayed with it, pushing his cock into her and grinding his pubic bone against her clitoris.

'I'm coming,' she cried as he felt her whole body tense under him. 'Oh my God, I'm coming . . .'

With one final spasm she arched off the bed and held his cock deep inside her. He pushed deeper still and felt her body trembling around him, every nerve responding to her climax. Then he felt her relax as though melting under him.

'Now it's your turn, lover,' she whispered in his ear.

He started a rhythm that was good for him. She made no attempt to change it but fitted herself to him. Her cunt was hot and wet and she whispered in his ear again, 'Give me your spunk, lover, I want it all.'

He could feel his spunk in his cock now. There was no reason to hold back but he did. He wanted to make her come again, force her to orgasm before he spunked. He quickened his pace. He sent his hand down between their two bodies so the tip of his finger could find her clitoris and wank it while he plunged in and out with his cock. She started to gasp with pleasure. He wanked harder and could feel her body respond. With his other hand he felt for her nipple under the material of the bra and pinched it hard. She started to whimper and then moan. Then she was screaming and he felt her cunt tense around his cock and heard her give one long, heart-felt cry as her third orgasm racked through her body.

He quickened his pace. He felt her hands on his buttocks urging him forward and he knew he could not told back any longer. He concentrated on himself now. He thrust into her as deeply as he could and felt his cock spasm as it pumped his hot spunk out into the soft clinging wet walls of her cunt.

'Bravo, bravo, bravo,' a man's voice was shouting.

Jason twisted round to see George Mason lolling in the chair by the desk. How long he had been there Jason did not know.

'Don't mind him, lover. George loves to watch. That's about all he's good for. And you certainly gave him his money's worth.'

He was glad he lived alone. After getting back from the Dorchester he was exhausted and cross with himself. He had blown it. His first chance at a big Hollywood film and he had ended up screwing the producer while the director watched.

Both of them had probably been so drunk they wouldn't even remember his name in the morning. And he could hardly ring up his agent and tell her what had happened. Fortunately he was so tired sleep overtook him the moment he got into bed and he was spared further self-recrimination until the morning.

He woke at nine. He trudged over to the curtains and threw them back, not really wanting the day to begin. Outside in the street a black Rolls Royce Phantom was parked. He wondered if someone in the street was having a royal visit as it was certainly unusual for this area, which, though far from depressed, was more used to second-hand Porsches and third-hand Range Rovers. Perhaps one of the royals was having a fling with a local resident, he thought, as he put on the coffee.

The doorbell startled him. He was not expecting anyone especially not at this time in the morning. He scrambled into a robe and went to his front door. He was even more startled to see Camilla Potts.

'Morning. Late night?' she asked knowingly.

'What are you doing here?' he was too astonished to be polite.

'Aren't you going to invite me in?'

'Sorry. Come in. I'm just surprised to see you.'

Camilla walked into the flat, found the front room and sat down on the sofa.

'Why?'

'Why am I surprised?'

'Yes. I thought Hanna told you.'

'Told me what?' Camilla's short skirt revealed a distracting amount of long lithe leg.

'She didn't. I thought she was a bit pissed. She wants you to screen test for the film.'

'What? Today?'

'Oh no, next week. But you have to leave today.'

'Leave?' Jason's mouth was wide open. This was all happening too fast.

'For Hollywood. Los Angeles. You know, where they make films. She didn't tell you?'

'No. Nothing. You mean leave now?'

'Twelve o'clock flight from Heathrow. We'll take you back to the Dorchester to pick up Hanna and you're off. You're flying with her.'

'How long will I be gone?'

'Depends on the screen test. You don't need to pack much. Hanna'll buy you everything you need out there. She likes doing that.'

He wanted to pinch himself. It must be a dream. He pretended he had to go to the loo so he had a moment alone to think. He had to call his agent. Talk it over with her.

'Don't be long,' Camilla shouted. 'We haven't got much time.'

Well, there was nothing else he could do but go with the flow. He went into the bedroom and pulled on his best jeans, a clean shirt and stuffed a couple of books and his shaving gear and a toothbrush into a briefcase. He walked back into the living-room, where he'd left his leather jacket.

'I have to call my agent.'

'There's a phone in the car, use that. It'll save time.'

He looked around, trying to think what else he should do.

'Cancel the papers. Turn off the electricity at the mains and the gas . . .' Camilla said helpfully. 'Write a note for the cleaning lady.'

'Don't have one,'

'Let's go, then.'

Camilla Potts was one of the most beautiful women he had ever seen, Jason decided as the chauffeur guided the Rolls Royce effortlessly through the traffic. The tight, short red dress she wore perfectly complimented the marvellous body he had seen so graphically exposed last night. The material moulded itself to her heavy breasts and amply curved hips. He could not help thinking, as it was positioned only two or three feet away, of her immaculately shaven – he assumed that was how the hair had been removed – cunt nestling no doubt in soft silk knickers under her skirt.

It was as if she read his thoughts. 'I prefer it. It makes me feel more open. More available. I like to feel available.' He laughed. 'Or do you like to think you've made a conquest?'

'I don't think so.'

'Good. That's so old fashioned. Women should be able to take the initiative. I'm glad you impressed Hanna. I was thinking about you last night. You bursting in on me like that. It was a turn on . . .'

'Was it?'

'Yes. It still is.'

She took his hand and pressed it into her lap. The tips of his fingers were inches from the top of her skirt.

'Do you want to call your agent?' she asked, unhooking the car-phone from its mounting and handing it to him.

'Thanks.' He dialled the number then returned his spare hand to Camilla's lap. She looked pleased.

'Hi. It's Jason MacIver,' he said into the phone.

'Hi, Jason, I'll put you through,' the receptionist said perkily.

'Jason.' It was Joy Chivas in person. Something must be up. 'Hanna Silverstein called me. She's offered me a deal for the film subject to a screen test.'

'Should I go, then?'

'Of course.'

Camilla Potts dropped to her knees on the thick wool carpet of the Rolls and pried his legs apart. Her hand reached for his zip.

'What about a contract?' he tried to concentrate.

Camilla extracted his cock from his pants and was stroking it enthusiastically. He could feel it growing in her hand.

'I'm still haggling. Don't worry, I'll work it out,' Joy was saying.

Camilla lowered her head and took his cock into her mouth. It was getting very difficult for Jason to concentrate on the phone call.

'What about . . . oh . . .' Camilla sucked voraciously, 'expenses.'

'Everything's paid for. First class travel. The works. Enjoy yourself.'

'I am . . . I mean, I will.' His cock was fully erect now and Camilla was using her tongue to lick every inch of it.

'Call me from LA.'

'OK,' he said, only too grateful to be able to throw the phone on to the seat. 'What are you doing? People will see.'

'I thought it was obvious what I was doing,' she said without taking the cock out of her mouth. 'And they can't see. The windows are black.'

She dived back on to his cock, pushing it so far into her mouth he thought he could feel her throat. He was generally dazed. Everything was happening so fast. He was on his way to Hollywood in a Rolls Royce Phantom whose interior was bigger than most people's sitting-rooms while the most beautiful woman he had ever seen was kneeling between his legs giving him a blow job. No wonder he'd wanted to be an actor! But what should he do now? Throw Camilla to the floor of the car and fuck her over the transmission tunnel or lie back and enjoy himself?

Camilla settled his dilemma. 'Relax,' she said. 'I want you to come in my mouth.'

'What about you?' he said gallantly.

'I want this.' She plunged her mouth back down on to his cock and began a relentless rhythm alternately sucking his cock in, then pulling it out of her mouth, her tongue flicking at the tip of the swollen rod of flesh, coating it with saliva both on the way in and on the way out. Meantime her hand had found its way into his trousers and was successfully massaging his balls and the stem of his cock. He felt the spunk rising in his prick. He opened his eyes to watch Camilla's head bobbing up and down on his cock. He could see that her other hand, the one not occupied between his legs, had insinuated its way between her own, pulled her tiny red briefs aside and was wanking her clitoris as vigorously as her mouth and hand were wanking his cock. Her skirt had ridden up over her bum and he could see her shaven pussy again.

There was no holding back now. He managed to mumble, 'I'm coming,' before he reached out and held her head down on his cock, not wanting it to pull back again. He wanted to spunk deep in her throat. Camilla reacted instinctively, sinking her head down deeper on him, deeper than he'd ever have thought possible and he felt her lips grazing his pubic hair. Her final thrust made him come. It was as though she'd contracted her throat muscles, squeezing his shaft. He moaned as he felt his spunk rocketing from his cock, so much he thought she would drown in it, as it hit the back of her throat. She swallowed it all except a drop which escaped from the side of her mouth and which she caught with the tip of her finger. She licked the finger clean, sucking it down into her mouth with obvious relish while she looked straight into his cold blue eyes.

'Welcome to Hollywood,' she said quietly smiling, as the Rolls Royce turned into the forecourt of the Dorchester. 'I must remember this. Good set-up. Might come in useful in my next epic.'

What this remark meant Jason had not the slightest idea. But now, he decided, was not the time to ask for an explanation.

# Chapter Two

It took an hour before the Rolls Royce and a second, less prestigious car, was loaded with Hanna Silverstein's luggage and Hanna herself replaced Camilla on the leather seat in the back next to Jason. As the chauffeur pulled into Park Lane and headed for the airport Jason was a little disappointed to learn that Camilla was not coming with them but apparently would be in Los Angeles in a few days' time. Meantime, she told him cryptically before Hanna arrived, she was sure he would have plenty to keep him occupied.

'I need a drink,' were Hanna's first words to him that morning. 'Pour me a Jim Beam straight, there's a good boy.'

Hanna appeared to like white. Last night she had worn a white dress and this morning she was wearing a white suit, with a white silk blouse underneath. Her shoes were white as were her tights.

Jason opened the large cocktail cabinet mounted in the centre of the partition between passenger and driver. Behind the beautiful walnut veneer was an amply filled bar stocked with every conceivable beverage. He poured the bourbon into a crystal tumbler and was about to add ice from a silver bucket recessed neatly into the side of the cabinet, when Hanna snatched the glass from his hand.

21

'Straight,' she said, as though explaining to a seven-year-old. She gulped the drink down. Its effect was dramatic. Hanna seemed to recognise Jason for the first time. 'Well Jason, we're on our way. Did Camilla fill you in?'

'A bit.'

'Lovely girl, isn't she? Gorgeous.'

'Yes.'

'She's got quite a reputation in Hollywood.'

'She's an actress?'

Hanna laughed huskily. 'She thinks so.' Hanna put her hand on Jason's knee and patted it. 'I really like you, Jason. You'll go far.'

'What about George Mason?'

'Oh, don't worry about him. He's not important. I make the decisions on my films. George couldn't discover talent if it was pushed up his anus.' She downed the rest of the drink and held out the glass. He refilled it.

'Such a strong face, Jason. They're going to love you in the States. You've never been there, have you?'

'No, I'm very . . .'

'They're going to love you,' she cut in before he could finish. 'I'm never wrong about these things. I'll get the screen test set up the moment we get in. You'll stay with me in Beverly Hills, of course. I've got lots of room and it's much better. We can work on the script . . .' She laughed and shot her hand out to grab at the top of his thigh and pinch it quite hard.

'Could I see a script?'

'What script?'

'The screen test . . .'

'Oh, that. The script's in rewrites. First draft was crap. To think I paid a hundred and fifty thousand dollars for that piece of shit. Jesus. Total crap . . .'

'But I thought you were going to start shooting . . .'

'Jason, you've got a lot to learn. We get a rewrite. It's being done now. No problem.'

'But my character . . .'

'Your character is a big strong horny stud who all the girls are mad to get between the sheets with . . . You can do that, can't you?'

Considering what had happened last night he thought it better to let actions speak louder than words. She knew what he could do. And so did George Mason.

'What's the plot?'

'No more business now, Jason. I've spent a week talking business with a load of schmucks and I want to relax. I like flying. It makes me high . . .' She laughed, suddenly realising what she had said. 'Give me another.'

He poured the Jim Beam. Just as he was taking the bottle away she caught his hand and tilted it up again, holding it until the glass was more than half full.

'Remember,' she said, 'that's how I like my drinks.'

The conversation lapsed. Hanna stared out of the window as they passed the Brompton Oratory and the Natural History Museum.

'So you like Camilla?'

'She's very beautiful.'

'And gives great head . . .'

Jason felt his face starting to redden. He was sure Camilla hadn't had time to tell Hanna what had happened in the car. They had only exchanged a few words outside the hotel. Or had she been acting on Hanna's instructions? In this new world in which he found himself anything was possible.

'Of course, you wouldn't know, would you?' she said. 'Not over here.'

He didn't know what that meant either. He wanted to ask how she knew of Camilla's capabilities. But he said nothing: it was better to look, listen and learn.

Two hours later they were installed in the spacious seats of the first class cabin on the upper deck of a Boeing 747 Big Top, and being plied with glasses of champagne, prior to take-off, by an extremely pretty stewardess.

Jason, who had drunk nothing in the car, accepted a glass willingly, feeling it was appropriate. Hanna refused.

'Bring me a Jim Beam, dear. Large. Extra large, honey. And keep it coming. You understand?' She caught the blonde stewardess's hand and looked into her eyes as if she was just about to tell her the secret of life.

'Yes . . . Ms Silverstein.' She read the name from little tags pinned in the top of each seat.

'Great.'

Hanna had consumed most of the bottle of bourbon in the limousine, two extra-large measures in the first class lounge while they waited for the flight to be called, but still downed the glass the stewardess brought as though she had been in a desert for a week.

Only the imminent take-off prevented her from consuming another before they had left the ground.

The stewardess returned to relieve them of their glasses as the plane taxied up to the queue of aircraft waiting on the runway. She caught Jason's eye as she took Hanna's glass, her expression a mixture of amusement and pity. He raised his eyebrows, wanting to tell her Ms Silverstein's condition was nothing to do with him. He didn't know whether the message was understood.

As soon as the plane was airborne the stewardess brought another bourbon just as Hanna was searching for the call button to ask for one.

'Now that's what I call service,' Hanna declared. The pressurisation of the cabin seemed to have increased her intoxication considerably. 'Bring me two blankets and another bourbon and that's it . . . no food . . . no hot towels . . . nothing. Understand?' Her words were slurred.

Five minutes later, handing the empty glass to Jason, Hanna curled her small frame into a fetal ball, covered herself in the red airline blankets and within seconds was sleeping peacefully.

Jason got up quietly and went to find the galley. The crew were busy preparing lunch but the blonde stewardess came over immediately to relieve him of the glass.

'Thanks,' she said. 'If you'd rather sit alone while you're having lunch there's a spare double over there. Help yourself.'

'Good idea. I think she's out for the count.'

'Oh, it happens. We get a lot like that.'

He read the name tag on her uniform, pinned above her firm jutting bosom. 'Melanie, nice name . . .'

'I'm glad you think so,' she said, for a moment letting him see that this was not an official remark, part of her duties. 'Better get back,' she added, moving down to rejoin the feverish activity among her colleagues.

Jason sat on the aisle seat in the row she had suggested. He was glad not to have to worry about disturbing Hanna while he ate his lunch, especially as he was ravenously hungry. All the excitement – sexual and professional – had clearly affected his appetite.

He had never been in first class before so was not expecting the lavish cuisine. Smoked salmon, foie gras, Iranian caviar, a chateaubriand carved by the seat. There was vodka with the caviar, which he declined, and fine claret, which he drank appreciatively. A selection of cheeses was followed by an elaborate dessert and the offer of liqueurs. He was persuaded to have a small Armagnac with his coffee. If this was going to be his life from now on he certainly wouldn't be protesting. If it wasn't, he was determined to enjoy it while it lasted. After all, he could soon be on the next plane back home.

He scolded himself for that thought. He must think positive. He was going to make a huge success of his screen test. End of story.

The alcohol made him sleepy. He closed his eyes. He could still feel Camilla's lips on his cock, her throat sucking him down . . .

'More coffee?' Melanie interrupted his reverie. She had been serving on the opposite side of the cabin so he had not seen her during the meal.

'Oh no . . . No thanks.'

She was looking down into his lap. He realised he had an erection. Is that what she was looking at?

'Let me take your napkin away, then.'

Before he could protest she dropped her hand on to the white linen and gripped it tightly, catching his cock in its folds. She smiled innocuously, gave another little squeeze, then plucked the linen out of his lap.

'I . . . eh . . .' he was trying to think of something to say to explain his condition.

'It's the vibration of the plane. Very common in our male passengers.' She smiled a knowing smile. 'Sometimes has the same effect on women but it's less noticeable. It always affects me.'

'Does it?'

'Always. Perhaps that's why I love my job. I'm on my break now for an hour. Do you feel like a little walk? Might help to relieve the discomfort . . .'

'A walk?'

'This is a very big plane. There are all sorts of places the passengers don't see. Trust me.'

'I do.'

'Come on, then.'

She picked up the tray containing the remnants of his meal, dropped the napkin on to it and lead him to the galley where she deposited the detritus. Her remarks had done nothing to lessen his erection. He put his hand in his pocket to press it against his belly. As he passed he saw Hanna Silverstein was still fast asleep, her knees practically touching her chin.

Melanie led the way up to the front of the plane. After the big meal most of the passengers were fast asleep or watching the individual video screens set into the armrests of their seats.

Next to the door leading to the flight deck was another door of exactly the same size. Both doors were marked in red letters STRICTLY NO ADMITTANCE – CREW ONLY. Looking around to see that no one was watching, Melanie took a key from her uniform pocket, more like a small spanner than a conventional key, and fitted it into the lock above the door handle. She opened the door quickly and shepherded Jason through. She checked again that they were unobserved before squeezing through the door herself and locking it after her.

Jason found himself in a narrow passageway packed on all sides with metal shelving containing various pieces of equipment obviously connected to the plane's complex computer systems. It was a bit like being inside the middle of a radio. Machinery clicked and hummed and buzzed. He could see little bright lights flashing as information was displayed on read-outs on the flight deck just the other side of the thin partition.

'Amazi . . .'

Melanie put her hand to his mouth to stop him finishing the word then put her finger to her lips to indicate the need for silence.

She led him down the short passage. To his astonishment, set in the middle of the available space, was the metal door of a lift. Melanie pressed its call button.

She could see his surprise and again put her hand across his mouth to prevent him blurting out, 'It's a lift.'

The lift arrived. The metal door slid open. There was just room for two. They eased inside. Jason saw there were three buttons on the control panel marked FD, MP, and CH. Melanie pressed CH and the door slid closed. The lift descended. She took her hand from his mouth.

'Now it's safe . . .' she said.

'A lift!'

'You guessed.'

'On a plane.'

'All the Big Tops have them.'

'Three floors.'

'Flight Deck, Main Passenger, Cargo Hold,' she explained.

The lift arrived at its destination. The door opened and Jason gazed out into the belly of the plane, stacked with aluminium wedge-shaped containers of cargo. He was about to get out when Melanie pulled him back. She pressed a button on the control panel marked HOLD. The lift door closed but the lift remained stationary.

'Now we are perfectly private,' she said. 'That button immobilises the lift. Good, eh?'

'What about the cargo hold? It's bigger . . .'

'It's also freezing. Access is only for emergencies. It's quite cosy in here, isn't it?' She pressed herself against him.

'I suppose so.'

'This is where members of the flight crew join the Mile High Club, Mr MacIver.'

'Jason.'

'Jason. Now, I can tell you what the initiation ceremony involves . . . or would you rather go back to your seat?'

'Initiation?'

'Into the Mile High Club. It's a very exclusive group. We have to set certain standards . . .'

Jason's astonishment and amazement were beginning to give way to a more basic instinct. Here he was at thirty-five thousand feet doing six hundred miles an hour in a lift the size of a telephone box with a gorgeous blonde. He was entitled to be a little taken back. Now, however, it was the feeling of Melanie's body against his that demanded his attention.

'This is all a bit fantastic.'

'But true.'

'So what do I have to do for my initiation?'

'First you have to kiss me,' she said.

That was easy. He'd wanted to do that since they'd first got into the lift. Melanie had one of those kissable mouths. Big fleshy lips, soft, welcoming. He pushed her against the lift wall and ground his mouth into her, flattening his body against her rich feminine curves, pushing his tongue deep between her lips and feeling hers, in turn, vying for position. His erection hardened again, pressing into her belly. Knowingly she pushed her navel against it, swivelling her hips so she moved across its length.

Jason lost himself in the kiss, feeling her body respond. It was a long time before they came up for air.

'Well,' she said, 'you've passed the first test with flying colours. Do you want to go on?'

'What do you think?'

'The next part is considerably more difficult.'

'Good,' he said, not in the mood to be teased.

'Kneel then,' she said.

'Kneel? In here?'

'I'm sworn by a secret oath to the Flight Crews Association that a passenger may not become a member of the MHC unless and until they have been through the prescribed initiation. It's a very serious matter . . .' Her eyes, a greeny blue, sparkled with pleasure. The tip of her tongue played with her upper lip.

'You could always make an exception . . .'

'Kneel or it's back to your seat.'

He slid to his knees. There was just enough room but with little to spare. His face was pressed into the pale blue serge of her uniform skirt.

Slowly, very slowly, with her hands on her hips, she inched the skirt up over her legs. Though it was quite tight-fitting at the front and back the skirt was pleated at the side to make it more comfortable to work in. Slowly the material slid passed his face to bunch at her waist and he was confronted with the flesh coloured nylon of her tights over which she wore a pair of tight high cut white panties edged with lace. He could see no stray pubic hairs.

Suddenly he was plunged into darkness. She had taken the skirt and pulled it down over his head so it draped over his shoulders, burying him in her thighs.

'Now you have to take my knickers down, Jason . . .'

Eagerly he reached up with his hands. She slapped them down. 'No, no. Put your hands behind your back.' Her voice was muffled by the skirt around his ears. 'It's the rules, Jason. You have to use your teeth.'

He hesitated, then locked his hands in the small of his back. In the dark he could smell the musky aroma of her sex. It was heady. He would have done anything she asked. This was exciting.

Groping forward with his mouth he felt the hardness of her pubic bone and the silkiness of her panties. He used his tongue to guide him, feeling the precipice as the bone curved down between her thighs. Here he turned his head sideways and gently, not wanting to catch her soft labia between his teeth, edged his tongue under the hem of the panties. To his puzzlement instead of feeling the harshness of nylon tights there with his tongue, he felt instead the tickle of her pubic hair and the puffiness of her labia. He concentrated on pulling the panties away from her body after this momentary distraction. He felt them give.

'Very good . . .' he heard her say.

He brought his teeth to bear on the patch of silk he had loosened and bit on it tentatively. As there was no resulting squeal of protest he assumed all he had in his grip was material so he pulled sharply downward and felt the silk slide over her hips. It was not easy. It was hot under the skirt and his mouth made the silk wet and slip from his mouth. Each time this happened he had to grope around to gain a new purchase. Strangely all this made the task more erotic and more exciting. His erection throbbed.

As he worked the panties lower there was some light coming up from under the skirt and he could almost see what he was doing. Finally the panties fell to the floor of their own accord and on to her pale blue court shoes.

'You did it,' she said, pulling the skirt off his head. His face was covered in sweat, his hair tousled by the material. 'And now . . .'

She unzipped the skirt, let it fall to the floor, and stepped out of it and her panties. There was nowhere to put them so she hung them across Jason's shoulder.

'And now the final phase . . .'

By way of explanation she pushed his head into her navel. Now he could see why he had felt pubic hair under the panties and not the mesh of the nylon. The centre of the tights had been neatly cut away and hemmed to reveal the whole of the slit of her sex.

'It's a little modification members of the MHC make . . .' she explained as she pushed his head against her body. She opened her legs as wide as the confines of the lift would allow. In his short but active sex-life Jason had never seen a sex like

32

hers. The lips of her cunt were puffy to the point of protuberance. It looked as though they had been attached to a pump and ballooned up with air. Her whole sex seemed like a thing apart from her body, a separate being clinging limpet-like between her legs. The being was covered with a fine down of hair, so fine it looked like cashmere, but very short, almost like fur. It was beautiful and very sexy. He kissed it, like he had kissed her mouth, easing his tongue between the labia to find her clitoris. It was wet in there already. Very wet. Quicksilver wet, frictionless and silky.

'Yes, good boy . . .' she moaned as his tongue went to work. She never stopped talking from then on. 'Oh yes, there, there . . .' as his tongue found the tiny nodule of nerves. 'Like that, like that . . .' as he tapped it. 'Oh, oh . . . yes . . .' as he licked it. 'I love it, I love it . . .' as he dipped his head lower and strained to get his tongue into the opening of her cunt. 'Oh no, my clitoris, my clitoris, baby . . . make me come. I want to come on your tongue. Do it to me. Make me come in your mouth. Then you can fuck me . . .'

His tongue went back to her pink raw flesh and found the swollen bud of her clitoris, a tiny island in a sea of flesh. He flicked it from side to side feeling her body tremble as he brought his hands up and around her thighs to hold her buttocks firmly, making his fingers into claws and digging them into the nylon-covered buttocks. Then he took up a tempo, round circles, boat trips round the island, round the lighthouse at the centre of her feelings. Hot wet circles with his tongue.

She gasped. Suddenly he felt her whole body tense. 'Don't stop,' she screamed, 'for God's sake don't stop, don't stop . . . don't st . . .' Her body convulsed. He felt her labia throbbing.

She made one final sound, like an animal, a sob that sounded like pain but was in fact relief, then all the tension left her body. Had it not been for the walls of the lift physically preventing her she would have slid to the floor.

She looked down at him and smiled. 'Under the authority invested in me,' she said solemnly, 'I am empowered to enrol you as a life-time member of the Mile-High Club.'

'Well, thank you . . .' he grinned.

'Which means you are now permitted to fuck me at thirty-five thousand feet.'

'And I always say, there's no time like the present.'

'Couldn't have put it better myself.'

He hauled himself to his feet in the cramped space. She reached for his belt while he struggled with the zip. In seconds his jeans and pants were around his ankles. There was no time to go through the contortions that would be necessary to get them off altogether. His need was too urgent.

Melanie looked down at his cock. It was wet with his own fluid, its circumcised head glistening. She started to drop to her knees, but Jason caught her by the elbows.

'No, I want your cunt . . .' he said bluntly.

Wrapping his arms around her waist he lifted her off her feet, her legs apart, and planted her squarely on the root of his cock. It went into her right up to the hilt, riding on the wave of her juices.

'Oh . . .' she squealed.

As he lowered her he went deeper still until finally the tips of her toes were on the floor. Not for long. Melanie had done this before. She knew how to fuck in a space not much bigger than a phone-box. She knew what to do.

Leaning back against the wall of the lift she braced her two feet on the opposite wall. Gradually with little steps she started working up the wall, Jason's upright body between her legs. As she went higher the angle of penetration changed until it was as though he were fucking her lying on her back with her legs raised in the air. She stopped when her thighs were at right angles to her body and braced herself. It took surprisingly little effort to hold herself steady.

'Clever . . .' he said.

'I want you deep. I want you to spunk deep. Give it to me. God, I'm so hot . . .'

He pulled his cock back almost to the lips of her cunt. He could feel their puffiness and their furry covering. He thrust forward slowly this time, feeling her cunt welcoming him, its silky walls clinging to his rod of flesh, sucking him in. He pulled back and thrust forward. He thought he could feel the rim of his glans against the walls of her cunt. His pace increased. He could no longer control what he did. Groping for her breasts, which he had not seen or touched, he felt the hardness of her nipple under the layers of material, her blouse and bra. He wanted to kiss her mouth but as he moved to find it with his, he felt his cock beginning to spasm and knew it was too late to do anything but feel, feel his spunk spitting out into the dark cave of her body, jetting out against the wet flesh in the depths of her cunt.

He buried his face in her neck. Her skin smelt sweet. His cock began to soften. It was the second time he'd come that day.

She walked her feet back down the wall and they both lent against opposite sides of the lift, silent, replete with feeling, enjoying the aftermath of orgasm as it played softly in their nerves, little tiny muted versions of what had gone before.

Snapping out of the trance Melanie looked at her watch. 'Christ, I've got to get back.' She picked her skirt off his shoulders and stepped back into it.

'I suppose you do this with all the passengers,' Jason said as he watched the neat furry pubis disappear under the pale blue skirt. In such a limited space they were obliged to co-ordinate their movements. He could not stoop to pull up his jeans until she was upright again.

'Oh yes, it's all part of UK Sky's unique passenger in-flight service. That's why they say our First Class passengers are given every comfort.'

'Well, I've certainly got no complaints. Perhaps I should write a letter of recommendation . . . Here.' He handed her the white panties.

'Keep them. Souvenir. Your badge of entry into the Mile High Club.'

'Thanks,' he said, stuffing the panties into his pocket.

'Don't mention it, I've got to get back.'

Melanie tried to comb her hair back into shape with her fingers using the reflective surface of the shiny metal door as a mirror. Then she performed the same service for Jason.

'I've never seen a man as blond as you before,' she said.

'Well, now you know it's natural.'

'What do you do for a living?'

'Actor. I'm going to Hollywood for a screen test,' he said. It was the first time he'd told anyone. He sounded good. It made it seemed real.

'Great! So I'll be seeing you in the movies.'

'You might. Only might. A lot could go wrong.'

'You'll do it. They must be impressed if they're flying you out first class . . .'

'We'll see.'

'Good luck, then.'

She pressed the button marked FD and the lift started to move smoothly upward. It was a strange feeling to be going up in a lift in a plane, Jason thought, but so was what he had just done.

Melanie put her finger to her lips again as the lift door slid open. They tiptoed passed all the humming computer equipment and she opened the outer door with her key. With the door ajar she checked that all was clear. Kissing Jason on the cheek and mouthing 'bye' she let him out. He made his way back through the main cabin, passed the sleeping passengers to sit next to Hanna feeling, now, like a doze himself.

He watched as Melanie appeared, locking the door after her. She winked at him before she went into the galley.

Hanna Silverstein woke up with a start. Jason hadn't dozed for long and was watching a movie on the video.

'I was dreaming about you,' she said in a tone of voice he had not heard her use before. It was soft, feminine and gentle. She put her hand on his knee as if wanting to reassure herself that he was real.

Jason wasn't sure how to respond to what sounded like affection. 'Really?' was all he could think of saying.

'Sure. I think it was a wet dream.' That sounded more in character.

Even more uncertain as to how to respond to this remark, Jason said nothing.

'Yeah. I'm always getting wet dreams. Just like a man, eh? You had this fucking great cock. I mean you've got quite a length on you anyway but this was like inflated.' Hanna's voice was coarse again, the momentarily gentleness gone. 'Feel . . .'

'What?'

'Feel.'

'Feel what?'

'Dummy,' she said. She took his hand by the wrist and pulled it under the red blankets that Melanie had given her. He could feel the accumulated warmth of her body. She tugged his hand up under her white skirt until it was at the junction of her thighs where the warmth was even greater. 'Get to work, honey,' she said, leaning forward so her head rested on his shoulder.

She pushed his hand against her tights. They were more than damp, they were distinctly wet. The movements of her body left him in no doubt as to what she wanted him to do.

'Wet, see . . .' she said.

'I can't . . .'

'Just a little attention . . . just give me a little attention, big boy.'

'People will see.'

'Everyone's asleep. No one's going to notice.' As if to confirm what she said she moved herself against his hand. Then with one leg still curled up on the sleeper seat she extended the other out straight. He saw her foot emerge from the blanket. She pressed his fingers into her now accessible sex. He could feel the wispy pubic hair flattened by the nylon of the tights. Apparently she wasn't wearing knickers.

For a moment he did nothing. His mind was spinning. Fucking Hanna Silverstein had got him this far. She appeared to be a very determined and resourceful woman used to getting what she wanted. If he refused to do her bidding now, what would happen? He might be on the next plane back home. If he hadn't objected back at the Dorchester is was hardly reasonable to object now. For the time being he had no choice but to play along, and put his foot down later when he'd definitely got the part.

'Come on, big boy,' Hanna prompted.

There was no alternative. Hanna was just too important to his future. He couldn't risk a row with her now.

He eased his hand up towards her navel until he felt the elastic waistband of the tights. Immediately Hanna lifted her hips off the seat allowing him to pull the tights down. He stopped when they were around her thighs. However slowly he moved he was sure it was quite obvious what was happening under the red blankets. There was a middle-aged couple sitting in the seats across the aisle. The man was asleep but his wife – she wore a large gold wedding ring next to another ring set with a ruby – was reading a book by the light of the lamp in the overhead panel. All the shades in the cabin were drawn but with bright sunlight outside it was dark enough to need light for reading, but not dark enough to hide what Jason was doing.

As soon as the tights were far enough down Jason moved his hand back on to her sex. He ran his fingers down into her labia. In contrast to Melanie's they felt firm and tight but the wetness he had felt on the nylon was reflected there. She was soaking wet.

'See, big boy, I do get wet dreams. And this one was all about you . . .'

His fingers parted the little hood of her clitoris and slipped on to the button underneath.

'Oh . . .' Hanna moaned.

The woman across the aisle looked over at them. She shifted herself in her seat.

'Sh . . .' Jason entreated.

He massaged her clitoris gently, trying not to provoke further outbursts. He felt Hanna respond, her whole body melting around the tip of his finger. He felt her trembling.

'Oh, so good . . .' she whispered. 'So good. I wish you could put your cock in there . . . that huge cock . . . stretching me till I couldn't take any more.'

He let his thumb take over the work on her clitoris while his fingers slid down to the mouth of her cunt. Hoping it wouldn't provoke another outburst he penetrated it with two fingers.

'Oh . . .' Hanna gasped louder than before.

The woman across the aisle looked at them again. She was in her forties and still attractive. Her figure was neat and trim. Jason looked over at her and she smiled wanly at him. She put her hand to her cheek, thereby being able to press her forearm into her ample bosom. She shifted in the seat again.

'You have to be quiet,' Jason whispered.

'I'm trying. Don't stop, that's perfect . . .'

Jason's hand worked relentlessly. He thrust in and out of her body with three fingers while his thumb nudged her clitoris from side to side.

'Perfect . . .' she whispered.

He could feel her body tense and knew she was going to

come. Her trembling had increased to the point where her whole body seemed to be convulsing.

The woman across the aisle put down her book. She stared at them unabashed. There was no way she couldn't have guessed what was going on. She moved both her hands to her face in an attitude of prayer allowing both her forearms to press into her breasts. She pressed her thighs together, tightly manipulating her thigh muscles to bring pressure on her clit. The crotch of her knickers had worked its way up into the crack of her sex. Normally it would have been uncomfortable. At the moment it was welcome.

Jason moved his hand faster. Hanna's hand moved down his chest to the waistband of his jeans. He had an erection but fortunately, so he thought, it was caught in the folds of the jeans and not very prominent. Hanna freed it, pulling at the denim until she made a space for its expansion, a hard thick rigid tube of flesh running the length of his flies. Jason could do nothing to stop her. She gripped it like the handle of some machine.

Then she came. Her body stopped moving and tensed. Every muscle locked. He moved his hand inside her one final time, worked his thumb against her clitoris with one last effort and then, he swore, felt a rush of juices over his embedded finger like a man spunking.

'My God . . .' she almost shouted. 'Oh . . .' Her legs scissored together, squeezing his hand.

The woman across the aisle had her legs pressed tightly together too, the crotch of her knickers cutting right into her clitoris. Her eyes were watching Jason's cock, under Hanna's hand. She wished it was somewhere else. She didn't think anyone heard her soft moan of pleasure.

Jason extracted his hand from the liquid centre of Hanna Silverstein. He tried, as best he could, to pull her tights back up into position, concentrating on making sure the blankets did not slip off as he did.

'Is there anything I can get you?'

He looked up in surprise at the sound of Melanie's voice. She was looking straight into his eyes. How long she had been watching he did not know, but her face was grinning so broadly that it had obviously been for some time.

'No thank you,' he said.

'A hot towel perhaps?' she suggested. 'Very refreshing.'

'No.' Jason felt like a boy who had been caught with his hand in the biscuit jar.

'Yes,' Hanna said emphatically. 'I'll have a hot towel. And you can bring me a large bourbon.'

# Chapter Three

With the time change, flying into the sun, it was the middle of the afternoon when the huge plane touched down in Los Angeles and it had been a hot day. But it was not until they had waited to collect Hanna's extensive luggage with the help of two burly black Red Caps that looked like they played defence for the Los Angeles Rams, and trundled it through the air-conditioned airport concourse to the awaiting limousine, that Jason felt the afternoon heat of the city.

Jason had seen stretch Cadillac limousines in films but had always thought there were exaggerated, constructed especially for movies. When he saw the size of the car the Red Caps were loading the luggage into he realised he had been wrong. The car was practically as long as a London bus.

Hanna climbed into the back and Jason followed. The interior was luxurious, but unlike the Rolls was finished in wood-effect plastic rather than French polished walnut. But it had everything. There were two phones, a fax machine, a television and video recorder, a CD player and a cocktail cabinet. The driver had left the engine running so the interior was cooled by the air-conditioning unit.

'Welcome to LA,' Hanna said as Jason sat beside her in the big leather seat. Her hand snaked out to pinch his knee.

'Unbelievable,' he said. So much was precisely that, he wasn't at all sure to what he was referring.

'What?'

'Everything. The car . . .'

'You can even get one with a jacuzzi.'

The driver tipped the Red Caps and got behind the wheel. Somewhere, it seemed like a long way away, an engine purred.

They drove past the strange structure that dominated the airport architecture, a building like a four-legged spider, with a revolving restaurant hanging under its belly, then headed out on a maze of slip roads to a four-lane freeway. In minutes they were in the city. Furniture warehouses, drive-ins – banks, fast food, laundries – lined the road. There were acres of bungalows. Nothing in this part of the city was more than one storey high.

'Sunset Strip,' Hanna announced as the car took a left at the top of a short hill.

They travelled down Sunset Boulevard and into Beverly Hills. The brash advertising slogans of the restaurants, hotels and apartment buildings gave way to the spacious grandeur of the houses of the super-rich. They passed the entrance to the Beverly Hills Hotel and Jason glimpsed the elaborate building at the top of a long driveway, surrounded by palms. Immensely tall, smooth-barked trees, sequoias Jason thought but was not entirely sure, lined the wide immaculately kept roads and pavements. Back, well back, from the road, behind front gardens the size of football pitches, stood various styles of house, American colonial with Corinthian columns, Spanish with arched gables, modern with walls of plate glass, all massive, all well separated from their neighbours by vast gardens and high fences.

As they progressed deeper into the hills and the road climbed higher, the houses became even larger, surrounded by walls with electronic security systems and high gates at the entrances to their driveways. The Cadillac slowed and turned into one such house, the driver operating a radio control to open the two wrought-iron gates electrically. It swept up the long drive to a large timber-framed house, the sort of style Jason had seen in films of the deep south, with a covered porch running the whole width of the front of the house, supported on a wooden frame and half enclosed by a white-painted picket fence. There was a swinging seat suspended from the overhanging roof. Jason half expected to see James Stewart sitting swaying lazily on its floral patterned cushions.

'Home,' Hanna said.

'What a place.'

'It's comfortable.'

The chauffeur swung the big car up to the front door and immediately came round to open the rear passenger door.

As they extracted themselves from the car – a Cadillac was not the easiest car to get out of, it was low to the ground and had little head room – the large panelled front door swung open and an olive-skinned woman in a plain black dress came down the steps to greet Hanna.

'Welcome home, Ms Hanna,' she said with a heavy Spanish accent. She smiled broadly showing her less than perfect dental work, her chubby face seemingly genuinely pleased to she her mistress.

'Thank you, Maria,' Hanna said.

The chauffeur began to unpack the luggage. Maria, her pear-shaped body thick with fat concentrated below the waist, started to help.

'Follow me,' Hanna said to Jason. 'I'll give you the guided tour.'

For the next half-hour Jason followed Hanna around the estate, his mouth gaping wider at each new note on the scale of luxury. At the back of the house French windows opened on to a paved terrace alongside which was an Olympic-sized swimming pool landscaped into the extensive gardens with one end formed into a rock pool and waterfall. There were two hot tubs set into the rocks here both with jacuzzis, Hanna explained.

'It's great when it's cold. Lie here under the stars in steaming hot water . . .' Hanna's tone was soft and lyrical for the second time in Jason's presence. This time it did not last long either. 'That is if you can see any stars through the smog . . .'

The gardens dropped away on a long lawned slope to a summerhouse, the size of a large house in itself, and garages neatly disguised by a bank of exotic shrubs. Hanna lead him into the garage. There was a Mercedes 600SL, a Ferrari Testarossa and a Range Rover as well as an American Ford station wagon. All gleamed as though they had just come from the showrooms.

'Use any one you want,' Hanna said. 'There's a board over there with the keys.'

Beside the garage were two tennis courts fitted with floodlights and a fully equipped gym with showers and two saunas.

'This is great.'

'I have a personal trainer. Comes and puts me through hell twice a week.'

Back in the house Hanna showed Jason through the kitchen

and spacious dining room to a private cinema, a perfect miniature of a real cinema complete with heavy velvet curtains over the screen and a steeply raked floor. About twenty plush seats were arranged on three levels. The seat in the middle at the back was fitted with a small desk from which a microphone on a flexible stalk projected, presumably connected to the projection box.

'This house belonged to Douglas Fairbanks. He used to watch his movies in here. Course I had it modernised some . . .'

Hanna lead the way to the front hall from which a sweeping staircase lead up to the first floor. They walked down a long corridor at the top of the stairs at the end of which was a set of double doors. Hanna threw both doors open.

'The master bedroom,' she announced. 'Except in my case it's the mistress's bedroom . . .'

The room was the size of a tennis court. Carpeted in a thick cream wool it was dominated by an enormous double bed covered with a white silk counterpane. The same material had been used to cover the walls. Two matching low-slung sofas were arranged opposite the bed, their upholstery an oatmeal wild silk that toned with the walls and the carpets. The whole room was decorated in a symphony of whites and beige. There was no clutter, no mess.

To one side of the room was a dressing room, crammed with clothes hanging on custom-made racks or in beautifully crafted yew drawers. One wall was covered with a rack for at least two hundred pairs of shoes.

'Tomorrow we have to get you some clothes,' Hanna said.

'I'm certainly going to need something,' Jason replied, trying not to feel intimidated by all this luxury.

Another door lead into the bathroom. A circular bathtub was set on a plinth in the middle of the room. To the side were two separate shower cubicles. The whole room was tiled in white marble with the exception of one complete wall behind the two matching wash-hand basins, which was covered from floor to ceiling in mirror glass.

'Well baby, that's the tour.'

'It's an amazing house.' That was an understatement.

'Treat it like home,' she said. She stripped off her jacket and unzipped her skirt. 'I need a shower.'

Her skirt fell to the floor, she stepped out of it, kicked off her shoes and walked into his arms. 'Run me a nice hot shower, big boy.'

She sat on a small stool in front of the wash basins which were fitted into a vanity unit, took out some make-up remover and started to dab off her make-up with cotton-wool balls.

Jason found the controls of the shower and turned the mixer tap, testing the temperature of the water with his hand. He felt distinctly uncomfortable.

Her face clean Hanna stripped off her tights, blouse and bra. He had not seen her breasts before. They were small, no more than crescents of flesh folded on top of her ribs, but her nipples were big, bulbous and red, bright ruby red. Her body was skinny, flesh stretched over bone. There was a yawning gap between her thighs even though she was standing with her legs together. Her tan, the colour of hide, was not spoiled by any bikini lines.

She climbed into the shower cubicle.

Jason wanted a shower too. Most of all, though, he wanted to ask where he should sleep and was afraid the answer was going to be right here in her bed. There were obviously lots of guest rooms in the house but he had no idea how to suggest he should be given one of them.

For a moment he contented himself with stripping his clothes off and using the other shower cubicle, letting the water soothe away the tensions of an eleven-hour flight.

When he stepped out of the cubicle Hanna had gone. He pulled on one of the white towelling robes that hung on the back of the bathroom door and went to look for her.

In the bedroom all the curtains had been drawn. It was getting dark now anyway so the room was shadowy, the only real light coming from a bedside lamp that Hanna had turned on. She had stripped the counterpane back and lay in the middle of the bed. She was wearing a white silk camisole, like a short nightdress. It made her tan look softer by contrast.

'You must be hot,' she said.

'Hot?' He sat on the edge of the bed, rubbing the robe against his body to dry himself.

'I mean, what I made you do on the plane. Not getting any relief yourself. It must have been terrible for you. Didn't you want to do it like crazy?'

'Yes,' Jason lied. Doing it like crazy was exactly what he had done.

'Poor boy. Poor big boy. Well, now I'm going to give you some relief. It's your turn. Lie back here.'

'Wouldn't you rather get some sleep? Aren't you jet-lagged?'

'Oh, we can sleep later. We've got all the time in the world. Let me do it to you, Jason, then you'll sleep like a baby. Besides, it's very bad for you to have all that tension in your body and not get relief. Didn't you know that?'

She had run her hand between her own legs and was strumming her labia like they were some strange musical instrument.

'I'm hot for you, lover boy. Hot for all that talent.'

Jason was trapped. He'd really rather have gone to bed. At least that's what his mind was telling him. His body had rather different ideas. His cock was making an appearance through the folds of the robe, like an actor appearing through the curtains, wondering if he should take another bow.

Hanna spotted it at once and applauded. 'See. I was right. Pent up frustration. Very bad for you.' Hanna got to her knees and pulled the robe off his shoulders. He finished the job, throwing it on to the floor. Immediately she pressed herself into his naked back. He could feel the soft silk of the camisole against his shoulder blades and under it her hard nipples.

Her hands wrapped round his deep hairless chest. She took his nipples between her fingers and pinched them quite hard. No one had ever done that to him before. He was astonished at the surge of raw passion that shot through his body. His cock swelled. Hanna felt it too.

'You like that . . .'

'Yes.'

She did it again. He shuddered with pleasure again.

Her hands dropped on to his cock and she circled it, wanking it gently. 'Lay back, baby, I'm going to give you a good time.'

Jason scrambled back on to the bed and lay on his back. The sheets were silk. He had never felt silk sheets before. Hanna stayed on her knees, the hem of the camisole just veiling the triangle of wispy pubic hair.

'So you've got sensitive nipples . . .'

Hanna lent forward and took the nearest in her teeth, biting it, licking it, sucking it, as though it were a woman's. Jason could not stop himself moaning with pleasure. Why hadn't anyone done this to him before? It was sensational. Hanna licked her way over to the other nipple and repeated the treatment. His nipples felt like they were connected directly to his cock, a single line of nerves, like an arc of electricity, every attack on them making his erection throb.

'So good . . .' he moaned.

'Oh I've got lots of tricks, big boy . . .'

She reached over to the bedside table and opened a drawer. She extracted a length of white silk ribbon about an inch wide. Jason raised his head to see what she was doing.

'You lie back. This is the speciality of the house.'

Hanna turned her attention to his cock. First she wrapped the ribbon under his balls and around the base of his hard shaft.

A tear of fluid had formed at its tip which she licked away casually with the tip of her tongue. She tied the ribbon tight and saw the veins in Jason's cock engorge, the blood trapped by the constriction. Then she took the rest of the long ribbon and wrapped it around his balls and up his thick shaft, as though bandaging it, one swathe after another, enclosing it right up to the rim under the helmet of his glans, so this was all that was left exposed. She worked the ribbon down again, covering what she had already covered then knotted it firmly under his balls.

'Here,' she said patting his cock. 'Feel good?'

'Yes . . .' he said tentatively. It felt like his cock was in the grip of a massive hand, which was holding it tightly along its length. By contrast the pink glans felt incredibly exposed.

Hanna reached into the bedside table again. This time she took, out a bright chrome chain, the same thickness as a dog leash but only seven or eight inches long. At each end Jason could see what looked like two shiny metal clamps, no bigger than a thumb, and attached to the chain by metal rings. Hanna climbed over his thighs, and positioned herself so her sex was poised over his rampant swathed cock.

She held the chain out for him to see. 'This is what you want, isn't it?' she asked.

'What is it?'

Smiling angelically at him she lowered herself gradually on to his cock. He felt her labia parting over the helmet of his cock as it nosed its way inside. It was hot and wet. She held herself above him when just his glans was inside her. He raised his head to look down his body. There, thrust between the V of her thighs he could see his cock wrapped in white ribbon. He didn't think it had ever felt harder in his life. His balls, tied tightly to his body, not loose and free as they usually were, ached from their constriction, but it was a marvellous, sexy, sensual, needy ache. They were full of spunk. He could feel it, despite the day's previous efforts.

Suddenly she dropped on him, the cock, ribbon and all, disappearing into her cunt, their pubic bones grinding together. She started bobbing up and down on him. Because his balls were bound to the stem of his cock it was as though she were fucking them too, as if trying to force them into her body, past her labia, into the wet sticky depths.

He had rested his head back, closing his eyes with the sheer pleasure. But the sound of the chain rattling made him look up. Hanna was fastening one end of the chain to her nipple. It was like a bulldog clip but more elaborate. He heard her moan as its jaws sunk into her tender flesh. She stopped moving, sinking down on his cock while she secured the other clamp to her free nipple. Another moan. The chain hung across her chest in a lazy loop.

Jason saw her eyes close. He felt her body shudder, her cunt contracting. Then she opened them again and he could see they were full of fire and excitement.

'Fuck me, big boy. Give me all that spunk. Come on, do it to me . . .'

She started riding up and down on him again like she was in the saddle of a horse. The chain across her chest bounced up and down, rattling, its weight making the clamps bite deeper into her nipples. She rode up, practically off his cock, then slammed down again. Up and down. Up and down until suddenly she stopped, dropping down on his cock, grinding herself down on it, trying to get it that millimetre deeper. She reached up with one hand and caught the chain between her breasts and pulled it down. The clamps bit deeper into her nipples, and that took her over the edge and down, plunging down into the black abyss of orgasm, her body trembling, her cunt spasming, her mouth open in a scream of pure pleasure.

Jason saw her release the chain. Her eyes opened again.

'You haven't come,' she said, not in anger but amazement. 'Well, you are a find. Real stamina. I like that, Jason. I like it a lot.'

Her fingers groped for the nipple clips. She took them off one by one. As each released her ruby red flesh she moaned and he felt her cunt contract.

Slowly she drew herself off his body, kneeling by his side. She trailed the chain across his chest.

'Well now,' she said, 'your turn.'

She positioned the first clamp over his nipple. Her other hand circled his cock. The ribbon was soaking wet. She began to wank him, first squeezing the exposed glans between thumb and forefinger, then, more conventionally, making her hand into a fist and using it to circle the white-ribboned shaft.

The jaws of the clip sunk into his puckered nipple. The edge of the jaws had little serrations like a row of tiny sharp teeth. He moaned with pain but it was pain so indistinguishable from pleasure that his whole body convulsed with an involuntary wave of sensation. He felt the chain snaking across his chest and the second clamp being positioned. She was wanking him faster and harder, the ribbon holding his cock in its unyielding grip too.

The jaws of the second clip bit into his nipple and that was that, that was all he could stand. The pain from his nipples, so close to the feeling of exquisite pleasure, arced, like electricity, to the infinite pleasure in his cock, and his whole body was consumed in sensation. He felt his cock spasm, pushing against its bondage and her cunning fingers, and his spunk shot high in the air, splashing down on his navel and thighs in big white gobs. It seemed to go on forever. Even after the spectacular fountain of spunk had ended its display, more seeped out from the little black slit of his glans and trickled down over Hanna's fingers.

'You needed that,' she said quietly.

She gently unclipped the jaws that held his nipples. She slowly unwrapped the ribbon that held his cock. She pulled a single sheet up over their bodies, after she'd dried him with a towel.

'You're going to be quite a success in this town, Jason. Believe me . . . I'm never wrong.'

With that she turned off the bedside lamp, turned on her side, nuzzled her tight bony arse into his thigh and went to sleep.

Jason didn't think he would sleep. It had been the most exciting day of his life and, because of the time change, the longest. There was so much to mull over and absorb, so much to think about. In fact he was sound asleep the moment he shut his eyes.

With jet lag, his body clock telling him that it was lunchtime when it was only six in the morning, Jason woke early, to discover he was alone in the bed. He got up, feeling ravenously hungry, and drew the curtains. The sun was already bright, the sky blue. On the vast lawns a squirrel was eating some sort of food.

Pulling on the white towelling robe that still lay where it had been dropped the night before, Jason headed downstairs. Wandering around he finally found the kitchen and a refrigerator the size of a wardrobe. He helped himself to orange juice and was just about to make a sandwich from the endless ingredients on the fully-stocked shelves, when he noticed that the large patio door that opened on to the terrace and the pool was wide open.

He went out into the early morning sun. The air was warm and pleasant. Hanna Silverstein, in a black one-piece swimsuit, was swimming up and down the pool. She was a strong swimmer, her movements economical and precise, hardly disturbing the surface at all, her body seeming to mould itself to the water. She swam the front crawl, her hands coming over her shoulders with absolute regularity, her fingers held together tightly to cut into the water like a knife, her face turning to breathe in the bow wave created by her head only every third or fourth stroke. At the end of each length she performed a proper spin-turn like a professional competitive swimmer, pushing off from the edge of the pool as hard as she could, letting the momentum carry her, underwater, for as long as it would, before she resurfaced and began the stroke again.

Jason sat on one of the many patio chairs and watched. It was always fascinating to watch someone perform anything with obvious expertise.

After twenty minutes Hanna pulled herself from the water. She looked radiant and young. Jason could suddenly imagine what she had looked like as a young woman.

'Hi, baby,' she said. She picked up a towel and wound it into her wet hair.

'You're such a wonderful swimmer,' he said.

'I should be. Used to swim for Georgia State when I was in college. Had a chance at the Olympics but never quite made it.' The pleasure of memory suffused her face.

'I thought you looked professional.'

'Sure. I swim a mile every day when I'm here. That and my training keeps me in shape.'

'Now I know.'

'Now you know. You hungry?'

'Starving.'

'Cook doesn't get in till eight. You want to risk my scrambled eggs?'

'Anything.'

'OK. Hand me that towel, will you. Hanna quite unselfconsciously stripped off the black swimsuit and towelled herself dry. Then she turned her back on Jason. 'Do my back, baby.'

He towelled her dry. The raised bones of her vertebrae looked like a relief map of a mountain range.

'You want to swim while I fix the eggs?'

'I'm too hungry.'

'Come on then.' She wrapped the towel around her body and they went into the kitchen.

She made him wholewheat toast and eggs and coffee. They sat at one corner of a large table on the terrace, the sun already beginning to feel hot on their faces.

Hanna ate nothing. She drank half a cup of coffee, went back into the kitchen and returned with a bottle of Jim Beam and a glass. She poured herself a large measure and drank it in one gulp. She poured another.

'Don't say it,' she said, reading Jason's expression.

'None of my business.'

'You've got that right.' She gulped down the second drink. The sourmash seemed to have soured her mood. The youthful, relaxed woman who had got out of the pool had become suddenly hard, her face lined in a frown. It was a remarkable transformation. She'd aged twenty years in front of his eyes.

Jason ate everything she had prepared. He finished the coffee too.

'So we'll get you clothes this morning.'

'I could have brought some. Camilla said . . .'

'I know what Camilla said. Come on.'

Hanna got up from the table and lead the way through the

house and back up to the bedroom. Maria, the pear-shaped housekeeper, had just arrived but Hanna did not acknowledge her 'Good morning'.

In the bedroom Hanna pulled off the towel from her body and the one around her hair.

'What do you think of my body, Jason?'

'It's great . . .'

'Too skinny,' she said, heading into the bathroom.

Jason looked around for his briefcase which contained his shaving gear and toothbrush.

'Jason . . .' Hanna called.

'Yes?' He walked into the bathroom. Hanna was in the shower.

'Come in here.'

It was an order, not a request. He hesitated. 'Get in here, Jason.' There was an edge of steel in her voice.

He walked off to the shower and peeled his robe off.

'Hurry up,' she said.

He stepped into the shower stall. The high pressure jet drenched him immediately.

'Go down on me, big boy. I need it.'

'Here?'

'Just do it.' Her tone left no room for argument.

She had her hands on his shoulders and was pushing him to his knees. Water cascaded over their bodies. He didn't want to do it. He was happy to go down on her, but not here, cramped and uncomfortable in the shower. As yet, however, he had not worked out a way to say no to Ms Silverstein.

As soon as he was on his knees Hanna lent back against the tiled wall of the shower and laced her fingers behind his head, pulling his face into her belly. Water splashed over her body into his eyes and nose. He licked at her wispy pubic hair. His tongue took on water. He had to get down lower to run his tongue into her sex but that was also where all the water ran off her thighs. Everytime he opened his mouth it filled with water.

She raised one leg, her thigh at right angles to his body. It made it easier. His tongue found her labia. If she was excited and wet it was impossible to tell. The water diluted her juices, washed them all away. She put her thigh on his shoulder. He found her clitoris. It was difficult for him to breathe. Water filled his mouth and nose. His knees were sore on the hard tiles of the shower floor. She slowly raised her other leg. With both her hands above her head she grasped the metal fitting that held the shower head, then hooked her other thigh over his shoulder, angling her cunt vertically into his face. Now he could get at it properly.

But he was angry with the discomfort. Reflecting his anger he raised two fingers to the mouth of her sex. He worried them against the dry lips, not caring if he hurt her. Finally they penetrated. Inside, past the outer ring, where the water couldn't penetrate, she was wet. She moaned.

He took her clitoris into his mouth, its little hood, its labia, everything, sucking it all in, sealing it so the water couldn't get in too. Then he found the centre of it and tapped it as hard as he could with his tongue.

She moaned again. He looked up into the stream of water as best he could. Her face was thrown back, her knuckles white as they clung to the metal fixture. Water cascaded over her body, her hair plastered down by it.

He pushed his fingers deeper, sucked harder, tapped and nudged with his tongue more brutally and felt her body tense. Her thighs gripped his head. She was coming. Deep inside her he felt her cunt contract. As he struggled to breathe through his nose against the endless stream of water, she shuddered to her climax on his mouth and fingers.

She lowered her legs. Jason sprang to his feet and turned off the water, gasping for air.

'I nearly drowned,' he managed to say.

'Don't be such a baby,' she scolded, still feeling the orgasm ebbing out of her body.

He staggered from the shower. How he was going to go about it he didn't know, but they were definitely going to have to have a serious talk.


The Cadillac deposited them on Rodeo Drive opposite the Beverly Wilshire Hotel.

'You'll need a couple of suits and a couple of sports jackets and slacks. Three or four shirts, socks, shorts . . .'

'Shorts?'

'American for knickers,' Hanna explained.

'If you could tell me a little bit more about the part I'd know what to look for,' he said.

'This isn't for the part, Jason. It's for wearing about town. The studio'll get your wardrobe for the test. We're having lunch with Martha Morris. You can't go to Ma Haute in jeans. Especially not in those jeans . . .'

Hanna walked into a large men's shop. Jason followed in her wake.

'*The* Martha Morris?' he asked.

'Of course, *the* Martha Morris,' Hanna replied testily. 'She wants me to give her a job.'

'She's been in all your films, hasn't she?'

'Most.'

'She's very good.'

'She used to be. She's over-exposed now. The public have got used to her three expressions. I'd rather find someone new. And she doesn't mean a thing at the box office any more. Her last two movies bombed.'

'Bombed?'

'Washed out.'

'She's still a big star, though.'

'Honey, you stick to what you know. That's good advice. Don't tell the engine driver how to drive the train.'

'Sorry.'

'Sure.'

A young shop assistant wearing a bright blue suit with an orange skirt came over to them, his sexual inclination written in his walk.

'Can I be of any help, Ms Silverstein?' he asked.

'You can.'

'It's a great pleasure to welcome you here again.'

'Oh sweet. We need suits, sports jackets, slacks . . . Something subtle. Nothing loud,' she said, as if commenting on the shop assistant's outfit.

'Of course, Armani I think. And St Laurent.' He rolled the 'aurent' in his mouth as if he were coughing. He was looking at Jason like he would look at a prize bull, while Jason wondered why Hanna was so well known in a man's shop.

'A few measurements, if the gentleman wouldn't mind,' the

assistant said, addressing himself to Hanna.

'Of course,' she said, without reference to Jason. It was as if he had ceased to exist.

The measurements were taken and Jason paraded for Hanna in a variety of suits, shirts and jackets. Every time he came out of the changing room Hanna and the assistant would discuss the merits of what he was wearing but he was never asked for his opinion. If he volunteered it, it was ignored.

'Oh, that's very sexy, don't you think?' Hanna said, when Jason appeared in a dark grey suit.

'Oh mucho macho,' the assistant agreed.

'We'll definitely take that.'

'I don't think it's . . .' Jason was about to say.

'We'll take it. Try the next.'

At the end of an hour they had everything Hanna wanted. Jason had not been allowed any choice though he had to admit most of the clothes were in superb taste and suited him. Since Hanna was footing the bill he felt his ability to complain was severely restricted.

'Knickers,' the assistant said. 'Shall I include some knickers?'

'He's only got what he came in.'

'Cotton or silk?'

'Cotton,' Hanna said.

'Silk is very nice against the peni.'

'Cotton's fine.' She winked at the assistant. 'He gets enough nice things against his peni.'

The assistant burst into laughter, making a mental note to tell his friend as soon as he got home that night. ('Do you know what Hanna Silverstein said?') Jason blushed. Hanna looked at him quizzically.

'Well, it's true isn't it, big boy?' she said, patting him on the cheek. 'Talking of which, he needs swimming trunks.'

Jason changed into the new Armani suit while Hanna went to the cash desk to settle the bill. The assistant packed up the other purchases and Jason's own shirt and jeans. He knocked discreetly on the changing room door.

'Excuse me, sir,' he said, the first words he had spoken to Jason directly.

Dressed, Jason came out of the cubicle. 'What is it?'

'If you take my advice, sir, I wouldn't let Ms Silverstein see these.' He held up Melanie's white panties. They had been in Jason's jeans pocket since the flight.

Jason blushed again. 'Dispose of them for me, would you?'

'All part of the service, sir,' the assistant replied, the panties disappearing immediately.

Back in the Cadillac, the Armani suit, Cerruti shirt and silk tie, and the Gucci loafers had not improved Jason's mood. His ire at the way he was being treated was increasing by the moment. He had come to Hollywood to be an actor, not to be treated like some glorified gigolo. Every time he had brought up the subject of work Hanna had fobbed him off. Well, after lunch he was determined he was going to put matters right. He rehearsed his speech as the car glided through the busy streets.

'Look, I find you a very attractive woman.' Very was a lie but it was diplomatic. 'But I'm an actor. An actor acts.' He remembered that line from *Tootsie*. 'I want to be in your film. I want to see the script. Even the old script would do. And I need to know when I'm getting the screen test so I can do some preparation . . .'

As soon as they got back to the house he'd tackle her. The

Cadillac drove along Sunset Strip up to Hollywood Boulevard passed Graumann's Chinese Theatre where footprints and handprints of the stars were set in cement in the pavements and up to Ma Haute, situated in a pretty garden on the edge of the Hollywood Hills. Each table had its own cane and canvas parasol protecting it from the direct sun.

Hanna had drunk bourbon on the way to Rodeo Drive and continued as they drove to the restaurant. She had said little to Jason and appeared moody and depressed. Erratic changes of mood were obviously part of her character.

'Darling!' Martha Morris said as the mâitre d' led them across the courtyard to what was clearly the best table in the restaurant.

'Darling!' Hanna replied. They kissed each other on both cheeks. Over Hanna's shoulder Martha's eyes fell on Jason. 'This is Jason MacIver. An actor from England.'

'Hello Jason,' Martha said, extending long, elegantly manicured fingers painted with a very red varnish.

'Hello, Ms Morris.'

'Martha, please,' she said at once.

They sat down at the table, the tablecloth a crisp white linen, the crockery white with a delicate blue motif consisting of the name of the establishment. A small bouquet of fresh flowers decorated the centre of the table, or as near the centre as the support of the parasol would allow.

Martha Morris was beautiful on screen. Jason had always thought so. He had seen a lot of her films. It was a shock to discover she was even more beautiful in the flesh. Martha was thirty-five but looked twenty-eight. Her flaming red hair was cut short to reveal the spectacular architecture of her neck, sinewy and long. The simple leotard top she was wearing revealed her fine arms and shoulders and a tunnel of cleavage below its V-neck. Her large breasts – he had seen them on screen in a long love scene she had done entirely naked – were the size of cantaloupe melons. Her figure was like an hour-glass, her waist waspie, her hips full and flared. Her long legs, hardly veiled by the short skirt she wore over the leotard, were slim and straight, her thighs delineated by the lines of her firm muscles, her calves narrow, her ankles pinched. Her complexion seemed to radiate health and fitness.

'Close your mouth, Jason,' Hanna said. 'You're catching flies.'

It was true. His mouth was open in wonder. Jason had watched the way Martha sat down, her movement so poised and graceful. He thought he should say something about her films. Apart from her beauty he'd always admired Martha professionally. He'd never seen her on stage, of course, but as far as film acting was concerned he'd always rated her among the best. He was trying to remember the last film he'd seen her in. It was a film of Hanna's directed by George Mason. But what should he say? 'I thought you were so good . . .' sounded like he was a fan, not a fellow professional, not an actor who might be working alongside her one day. And maybe one day soon. He decided to say nothing.

Hanna had grabbed a passing waiter by the arm, reeling him into the table like a fish on a line.

'Bring me a bourbon: large, straight,' she said, then looked at Jason. Jason looked at Martha's glass. She was drinking Perrier.

'Perrier, please,' he said.

'And a fucking Perrier.' She released the waiter from her clutches. 'This town used to be into booze. Now it's all Perrier on ice. Jesus, why doesn't anyone drink any more?'

'It's bad for you, Hanna. Haven't you heard?' Martha said.

'What, worse than all that snow people stick up their noses?'

'So they say.'

'Well, I prefer to take my drugs through my mouth.'

Jason looked around the terrace. There were at least two actors he recognised, one from films and one from television – a long-running police series. He thought he saw a member of the crew of the USS *Enterprise* but couldn't be certain since the man looked so old. Hanna was right, though. The tables were littered with bottles of mineral water, Perrier, Evian, Vittel and San Pellegrino, and several in shapes and colours he didn't recognise. The number of wine bottles or cocktail glasses he could count on the fingers of one hand.

'So how was London?' Martha asked.

'Cold, wet and expensive. Always the same.'

'It's summer there.' Martha protested.

'That makes a difference?'

'Have you been to England?' Jason asked nervously, his voice sounding squeaky.

'Sure. I made a film there about two years ago. At Pinewood. On the 007 Stage. Do you know it?'

Jason had never been to Pinewood. 'Oh yes . . .'

'Some piece of shit about a shipwreck. Like the *Marie Celeste*, you know. Anyway, after the first week they flooded the whole sound stage and I spent six weeks in and out of freezing water in a pair of panties and a torn blouse. It's a wonder I didn't catch pneumonia.'

She had turned to look at him as she spoke, looking straight into his eyes. She had deep green eyes. They sparkled with energy and life. They were the most beautiful eyes he had ever seen.

'So how's the script?' Martha turned the radiant orbs to Hanna. Jason felt as though he had been released from a hypnotic trance.

'I told you, darling, there's nothing for you . . .'

'You always say that. I had lunch with Bill Talbot. He told me there was a great female lead.'

'Bill Talbot would tell you anything to get into your knickers.'

'I don't think he's interested in anything quite that simple. Not from what I've heard.'

'Pity. Keep trying, though.'

Martha smiled innocently. 'I don't know what you mean.'

A waiter brought three menus, but Martha and Hanna waved theirs away. Only Jason took the huge white card. He was hungry again, his body clock telling him it was dinner time in England.

'Have the house salad,' Hanna said.

'I'm hungry . . .'

'It's great,' Martha added. 'They're famed for it.'

The waiter took their order. Hanna gave him her empty glass. 'And another Beam. Large.'

'That's why I'm here,' Jason said, wanting to join the conversation.

'Why?' Martha's eyes turned to him, their disconcerting power making him stutter.

'To . . . to . . . test for Hanna's film.'

'Really?' Martha looked interested. 'Have you read the script?'

'There's nothing for you, Martha. How many times do I have to tell you?'

'There's always something.'

'Not the lead.'

'I only play leads.'

'Exactly. So give it up.'

'Is it a good script?' Martha asked Jason, her long fingers touching his arm on the table.

'He hasn't read it.'

'I thought he was going to test . . .'

'Sure. But the script's in rewrites.'

The salads arrived, massive white plates with the restaurant logo, matching the side-plates, in the middle of which was a selection of green leaves: rocket, frissé, lollo rosso and endive, dressed in walnut oil and balsamic vinegar. Jason looked disappointed. This was hardly going to satisfy his appetite.

Hanna ordered another bourbon. Quite suddenly she appeared drunk. The booze seemed to affect her like this. She could drink continuously without apparently being affected at all and then, with no warning, it would catch up on her, as it had on the plane. Without much enthusiasm she picked over the leaves of the salad with her fork.

'This boy's great, incidentally,' she said, putting her hand out to pat Jason's upper arm. 'Great.'

'Really?' Martha said, smiling. Jason smiled too, assuming she meant his talent as an actor.

He was to be rapidly disappointed. 'Great. I mean a real good fuck. And gives great head.'

'Well, how nice . . .' Martha said, grinning.

'Sure. Big cock. Great stamina. Great buns. What more could a woman want. Eh Jason?'

Jason felt himself blushing. He knew Martha's eyes were looking straight at him.

'Quite a recommendation,' Martha said, laughing.

'Do me a favour darling would you?' Hanna asked.

'What's that?'

'I've got to get some sleep. I'm real tired. Jet lag, I guess. I'm going to take the Caddy home. Take care of Jason, would you?'

'Of course, darling,' Martha said. 'You all right?'

'See he gets home.'

'No problem.'

Hanna got to her feet unsteadily. For a moment Jason thought she was going to fall over but she kept her balance. She lent over and kissed Jason on the mouth. The kiss was sloppy and badly coordinated. Her tongue missed his lips and licked his chin. Leaving Jason she launched herself at Martha, kissing her cheek before standing upright, a little dizzy from her efforts.

'And if you want to fuck him, be my guest.' She said loudly. 'He's got plenty to go around.'

With most of the people at the surrounding tables looking round at this last remark Hanna set off across the terrace. The chauffeur, perhaps used to these sudden departures, was waiting by the entrance. Hanna more or less fell into his arms and was partly carried out of the restaurant.

Jason was fuming. In the whole conversation, apart from telling him what to eat, Hanna had not spoken to him once, treating him, as she had in the shop, as though he didn't exist as a person. That all this should have happened in front of

Martha Morris made it a hundred times worse.

'I think I should go,' he said. 'I'll get a taxi.'

'Stay.' She levelled those magic eyes on him, eyes that could not be refused. Her hand touched his forearm again. 'Hanna's the old-fashioned sort of producer, that's all. You mustn't be upset by her. She thinks actors are cattle. She treats everyone badly. There's even a rumour she had Robert Redford fired from a film because he wouldn't fuck her. It doesn't mean anything. The booze gets into her head and makes her crazy, is all.'

Whether it was what she was saying or those big eyes looking at him with such concern that made him feel better he didn't know but his spirits improved instantly.

'When did you meet her?'

'Day before yesterday.'

'See. You hardly know her at all.'

'I've seen most of her films.'

'There's a lot of rumours in the business about her. Private and professional.'

'Really?'

'Apparently. Things about how she's made so much money.'

'But her films . . .'

'Sure her films have made some. But she's never had a mega box office. Not big bucks. No *Jaws*, or *Home Alone*. That's where you make the big bucks. And she's got big bucks.'

'How, then?'

'It's only a rumour . . .'

'What?'

'That she's into porn.'

'Porn! But she's won awards. I mean, some of her films are classics. I thought she was one of the best producers in Hollywood . . .'

'She is. It's probably just rumours. Maybe she has a better deal with the studio than people think . . .'

'I don't know what I should do.'

'About what?'

Jason looked into her magic eyes and tried to decide what he should say. He badly needed advice. Martha looked sympathetic and caring and she was a fellow actor, after all, a fellow professional.

'What she said was true. She wants me to . . . I mean, we're sleeping together. She promised me a screen test. But she won't show me a script. Today she treats me like I don't exist. Like now. Perhaps I'm just being used . . .'

Martha laughed. 'Sorry . . .'

Jason was about to get to his feet. 'I'm going . . .'

'No.' She caught his arm. 'No. Stay. I'm sorry, Jason. Let me tell you something. This is Hollywood. Not Stratford-on-Avon. If you're into artistic integrity, go home. Here people fuck their way to the top. It's usually women, admittedly. But men have done it too. That's how it works here. If you don't like it then you'd better go home.'

'Is that true?'

'Sure. Practically every female star in this town and quite a few of the men. I did.'

'You?'

'Sure. I fucked every producer who'd even see me. I got a reputation for giving great head. Then they all wanted to see me.'

'I don't . . .'

71

'It's the way this town works. I've got a great body. I know how to use it. Course, these days I only fuck heads of studio. The more money you earn the more selective you become.'

For the second time Jason's mouth was wide open.

'Let's order coffee,' Martha said. 'You've got a lot to learn.'

She ordered decaffeinated expresso with a twist of lemon peel and Jason followed suit. They talked about acting and about films. In the middle of the conversation Jason suddenly saw himself, sitting in a famous LA restaurant, talking to a famous Hollywood star as though they were old friends. Three days before he had been packing shelves at Tescos. This whole experience was like a long and complex dream.

'Listen, Hanna's going to be out for the count all afternoon, I guess. Why don't you come up to my house. It's such a nice day. We could swim . . .'

'My trunks are in the Cadillac . . .'

'I've got spares.'

'I'd like that.' He looked into those gorgeous eyes. 'You've helped me so much. I was feeling like a piece of meat.'

'Right. It's a cattle market. You end up feeling like prime beefsteak.'

Martha signed the bill and they walked across the restaurant. A few of the women who had overheard Hanna's remarks eyed Jason speculatively, or was that just his imagination?

The car jockey saw them coming and disappeared at the run. A few minutes later a black open-topped Aston Martin pulled up to the curb. The car jockey jumped out and Martha dispensed a large tip. Jason climbed into the leather interior.

'Fasten your seat belt,' Martha said as she gunned the massive engine and the car surged out into the road.

# Chapter Four

Martha drove fast, her long legs expertly dabbing the pedals, while her hand worked the gear lever to keep the revs up. The tyres, on the hot tarmac, squealed in protest as they were forced around the steep winding corners in the Hollywood Hills. Gradually the whole of Los Angeles was spread out before them under a cloud of thick brown smog. It was a spectacular view, the city seemed to go on forever, as far as the eye could see.

The car pulled into the driveway of a small, at least compared to Hanna's mansion, low-built house. The garden surrounding it was a riot of semi-tropical plants. Martha pressed a control pad and the big double garage door swung open. She drove in, parking next to a white Cadillac Seville.

'Home,' she announced as the garage door descended again.

She lead Jason through the back door of the garage into a pretty landscaped garden completely secluded, with a large swimming pool as its centrepiece.

'It's beautiful,' Jason said. The many flowers seemed to have been planted in colour co-ordinated combinations so one corner of the garden was dominated by reds, another by shades of blue.

'If you want to swim you can change over there,' she said,

indicating a small wooden cabana half-hidden by a screen of foliage.

'What about you?'

'You go ahead. I won't be long.'

She let herself into the back door of the house. Next to it was a wall of glass patio windows.

Jason headed for the cabana. Inside he found a stack of towels and a selection of men's and women's swimsuits. Pulling off his new clothes and hanging them neatly, he tried on a pair of skimpy black trunks. They fitted perfectly. Diving into the pool he swam hard and fast, enjoying the exercise after two days of doing nothing. He worked himself hard, forgetting everything but the pull of muscle and the shape of his stroke.

It was half an hour before he levered himself out of the water. He did some press-ups and sit-ups on the patio and went back into the cabana to shower. He kept the swimming trunks on, dried himself with a towel, and walked into the house to find out what had happened to Martha.

Tentatively he walked through the spacious living room and into the kitchen. Both rooms were deserted. He reversed direction and found himself in the foyer behind the front door. A long corridor lay off to one side. The house was mostly painted white, its long walls hung with some notable examples of modern art. In the living room he had noticed a Lichtenstein, here in the hall there was a Rothko. As he walked down the corridor there were two Miros and a Kandinsky.

At the end of the hallway was a door. It was ajar and he could hear a voice though it was not forming words. The sounds were the little sighs and gasps of pleasure.

'Martha?'

'Come in,' she said, her voice husky and deep.

He pushed the door open. The room was dark, heavy curtains drawn across the big windows. But there was enough light to see Martha Morris lying on her back in the middle of a large double bed.

'Close the door,' she said. 'Where have you been? I had to start without you . . .'

Jason stood stock still, hardly believing what he saw. Martha was lying with her legs open, wide open, her knees bent. She was not naked. A tightly laced band of black satin hugged her body around the waist. It started under her breasts and extended to her navel. Attached to this were long black suspenders which snaked over her hips at the front and sides, to grip the welts of sheer black stockings, pulling them into peaks on her creamy thighs. Her breasts, big mounds of flesh, were pulled by gravity to either side of her chest, their nipples erect. But it was down between her legs that Jason's eyes were drawn. That was the only part of Martha's body he had not seen before in glorious Technicolor on a forty-foot screen. Her cunt was thick with red hair that had been carefully shaved so it would not escape a bikini. It was exactly the same colour as the flaming red hair on her head.

But that was not what Jason was staring at. Poking from the hair, like tusks from the mouth of some furry creature, were the stumps of two vibrators, one buried in her cunt and the other in her anus. The fingers of Martha's left hand bridged the gap between the two, holding them firmly in place, while one finger of her right hand was wanking at the top of the long slit of her sex, its tip pressing into her clitoris.

Jason had never seen a more erotic sight in his life. The

black corset seemed to emphasise the size of her tits and the swell of her hips, the stockings making her long shapely legs seem even longer. Somehow the whole outfit framed her sex, making it appear soft and open and vulnerable by contrast to the sleek, shiny, tight black satin, straining the laces that held it in place.

'Did you see that film I did in the nude?' Martha said, her voice breathy.

'Yes.'

'So am I better in the flesh?'

'You're sensational.'

'I'd hate for you to be disappointed.'

The finger on her clitoris moved from side to side. She moaned. 'Come here.'

She held out her right hand. He took it and felt it was wet. With surprising strength she pulled him down on to the bed and moved her head to kiss him, a long writhing wet kiss.

'Do it for me, honey,' she said. She took his hand and lead it down between her legs until he felt the hard phalluses. As soon as she was sure his hand was in place she took hers away. 'Do it . . .'

He wasn't sure he knew what to do. Like so much of what had happened to him in the last three days this was beyond his experience. Not that he was going to let that stop him. He pushed both vibrators further into her body. He got to his knees beside her hips so he could see what he was doing.

'Yes,' she said, as if confirming that was the right thing to do.

He looked closely at the long runnel of her sex covered in the thick ginger hair. The hair was damp. He heard Martha moan and felt the two vibrators slide outward, pushed by the contraction of her body. He pushed them back with one hand while he searched for her clitoris with the other. She moaned again as his finger found it.

'Oh honey, wank me . . . I love it . . .' she said, angling her hips off the bed.

He did as he was told, his finger wanking her clitoris as he pushed the vibrators home. With his fingers bridging both of them – as hers had done – he could not grip them enough to pull them out. That was her job. She contracted around them to push them out. Apparently that was what she wanted. He pushed them in and she used her interior muscles to push them out. He could see her doing it, her navel tensing, her face slack with passion. He tried to match the little circles he was making on her clitoris to the cycle of the vibrators, the inward thrust coming just as his finger reached the most sensitive apex of the tiny hooded knot.

'You're making me come already,' she managed to gasp.

She didn't need to tell him. He could see it. Above the bed was a huge poster of the film in which she had played a whore, the one in which she had stripped, the one with the long nude love scene. Her face in the poster, over-made up and tarty, looked down on them, its knowing expression matching the situation. Her body started to tense and she began to make a little sound, like an 'oh' but so regular it was more like panting for breath, or a dog barking continuously.

'Oh, oh, oh, oh, oh, oh, oh . . .'

He saw the muscles of her navel knit, pushing at the vibrators. Some instinct told him to take his hand away this time and let her expel them completely.

'Yes . . .' she said immediately.

The vibrator in her anus slid out first, the one in her cunt taking longer. He concentrated on her clitoris, her body rigid as an ironing board now.

'My God . . .' she gasped.

The vibrator in her cunt slipped out. She scissored her legs together, clutched the sheets with her fingers as though clawing for support, and moaned, her body shuddering uncontrollably. Jason watched as slowly the tension in her body slackened.

'Oh, so good,' she said, smiling up at him.

She sat up and started tugging the swimming trunks down. He co-operated. The trunks were so small his erection had already found its way out of the waistband. Immediately they were around his ankles, and with him still on his knees, Martha's mouth closed over his cock.

He could not help but gasp. He had experienced several women taking him in their mouths but never like this. Martha's mouth felt like a cunt. If he had not been able to look down and see her head bobbing in his lap, he would have sworn it was a cunt. It was hot and sticky like a cunt. It sucked him the whole length of his shaft like a cunt. It felt smooth and silky like a cunt and it took all of him, his whole cock. He could feel her lips at its base. He could feel her throat at its tip. The only difference was that, unlike a cunt, her mouth had a tongue, a tongue she was using expertly to drive him wild.

Her tongue was hot like fire. It licked his cock like an ice-cream, played with it, flicked at its tip on the outward stroke, reached for his scrotum on the inward. It seemed to be everywhere. He could have sworn it wrapped around him like a snake around a tree. He could hear her voice ('I got a reputation for giving great head'). Now he understood.

She pulled her head away, holding his saliva-covered cock in her hand. She looked into his eyes. 'You want to come in my mouth or do you want to fuck me? You choose, honey.'

A wicked smile played on her lips, just as it did in the poster above the bed.

Her free hand ran along his chest and on to his nipple. Until he felt her touch them he hadn't realised how sensitive they were. The clips that Hanna had applied had made tiny bruises. Martha's fingers provoked them. But once again, the pain charged the electricity of pleasure.

Violently, not thinking or caring, he pushed Martha back on the bed and literally fell on her. His cock pushed up between her legs and he was deep inside her before he really knew what he was doing. Her cunt was soaking wet. Again, with no thought, he started reaming in and out of her, feeling his own excitement coursing through his body, wave after wave of it. Everything he felt, everything he saw, or remembered, propelled him forward. The image of her lying on the bed, her legs crooked, the vibrators deep in her body, seemed to be burnt into his mind. The look in her eyes as he'd watched her come, the way her navel had tensed, the feeling of her mouth sucking on his cock. It was all there. All part of what he was feeling as he drove his cock into her.

But as his eyes rolled back and he suddenly stopped, finding his place in her body, feeling his cock taking him over, jerking his spunk out into the silky wet wallet, it was the feeling of Martha's sheer black stockings at his sides, her heels in his back, driving him still deeper into her, that finally made him come.

He was too involved in his own sensations to feel Martha's reaction to his frantic thrusts, but as his orgasm ebbed away he sensed he had driven her so close it would only need the slightest effort to bring her off again.

She clung to him, open, wet, wanton. Whether it was the same orgasm or another new one she did not know. But the relief when he drew his still hard cock back, then thrust forward again was enormous. He drove twice, using the last of his energy. It was enough. She came, feeling the wetness of his spunk inside her driven deeper by this second assault.

'Yes, yes, yes . . .' she said triumphantly as her whole body locked around the blackness of her climax.

Eventually he rolled off her, his cock flaccid and wet. Neither moved then. Jason felt his eyes close and an irresistible need to sleep overtook his mind. It was jet lag, no doubt. Or post orgasmic exhaustion, or both.

He woke with a start, for a second not knowing where in the world he was.

'Hi,' Martha said, her voice considerably less husky. 'Were you dreaming?'

'No . . .' he was still disorientated, the sleep had been so deep.

'You went right out.'

'Jet lag.'

'Could be.'

'How long?' His memory was returning. He knew where he was now.

'An hour.'

'Sorry.'

'Why sorry? You needed it. I slept too for a bit. It was very relaxing.'

Martha still wore the black stockings and the laced black satin corset. She had propped herself up on the pillows. Her big breasts were like perfect spheres; despite their size they sagged not at all.

'Do you want a drink?'

'Not yet.'

'Good.'

She rolled on to her side and down the bed until her head was level with his crotch. She kissed his hip then the side of his navel.

'I want to feel it grow in my mouth. I love that.'

She slipped his flaccid cock, balls and all, into her mouth. Almost at once he felt his blood pumping. Her tongue was licking the rim of his glans. It transferred to his balls. He closed his eyes, feeling his cock swelling. One of his balls could not be contained any more and popped from her lips. The other soon joined it, as his cock hardened to its full length.

Martha sat up, looking as pleased as if she'd raised the dead.

'That's better. Now, as they say in restaurants, there are two specialties of the house. You've just had one of them so would you like to go for the other?'

'You're spoiling me.'

'The truth is, I'm spoiling myself.'

She reached over to the bedside table where there was a jar of cold cream. Taking a good dollop in her hands she transferred it to the channel that ran between her breasts. She did not rub it in but moved both her hands to the sides of her tits, pushing them together to form a tight passage of flesh.

'In America we call this tit-fucking. So tit-fuck me, Jason,' she said, those magical green eyes staring at him with renewed excitement, as she lay back on the sheets.

He did not need any encouragement. Kneeling, he spread his legs on either side of her ribs and immediately thrust his cock into the white cream. She moulded her breasts with her hands and looked down to see his glans appearing from the top of her cleavage smeared with cream.

'Do it . . .' she urged.

He took up a rhythm. The cream spread over her breasts, up and down the length of his cock. She held her breasts firm. They were tanned and soft and made silky by the cream. Her face in the poster above the bed with its knowing eyes appeared to be watching him. In the poster most of one of her legs was showing through a split skirt. He looked from the poster to the real thing. He reached behind him, slipping his hand between her legs and finding her cunt. It was wet, a cocktail of her juices and his spunk.

'Make me a pearl necklace . . .' she begged obscenely, her face contorted in passion. He could feel her need in her cunt. Her whole body was alive, squirming and writhing under him. He felt her come, felt her cunt leap, her thighs squeezing together, trapping his hand, her body locked rigid. But her tits weren't rigid. They were soft and malleable, rich and plump. Jason was coming too, her orgasm provoking his, taking him over the edge as his cock thrust in and out of the two great mounds of flesh.

A string of white spunk shot out of his cock as it emerged from the top of her breasts for the last time. A pearl necklace of spunk.

Deliberately, waiting until his eyes had opened again, she gathered his seed with her finger. She brought her finger to her mouth and licked it clean, her magical eyes never leaving his. The finger made several journeys.

'Tastes so good . . .' she explained.

When she was satisfied she had finished the job Martha sat up. Slowly she unclipped the suspenders of the stockings and rolled them off her legs. Jason lay back, enjoying the view. She dropped each stocking on to his chest, then unlaced the black corset and dropped that on him too.

She got up and walked across the room, her tight arse swaying like a metronome. He heard the shower running.

'Hey, you'd better get going.'

She came back with a large pink towel wrapped around her body.

'God, it's seven o'clock.'

'I'll call you a cab.'

She sat on the bed and dialled for a taxi while Jason went to the cabana to retrieve his clothes.

By the time he had showered and dressed the taxi was waiting. Martha, still dressed in the towel, saw him off at the front door.

'So goodbye, lover,' she said. 'The taxi's on my account.'

'Will I see you again?'

'Sure. Here.' She handed him a little white printed card from a box on a table by the door. 'Call me any time.'

'Thanks.'

'And tell Hanna thanks for the loan. Oh, and that she was right.'

'Right about what? What loan?'

'You are a great fuck.' Martha smiled enigmatically and closed the front door.

Jason hoped she was teasing but there was something in the tone of her voice, and that smile, that made him think she was not. If she was serious he didn't like it, not one bit, not one tiny bit.

'Joy?'

'Hello, Jason. How goes it? You having a great time?'

The international connection between London and Los Angeles was crystal clear.

'Great,' he lied, though it was only half a lie. 'Listen, I need your advice.'

'That's what I'm here for.'

'Have you heard anything more about the deal?'

'What deal?'

'The deal for this picture . . .'

'We're still haggling.'

'That's what you said yesterday.'

'These things take time.'

'Have you spoken to Hanna again?'

'No. What's the problem, Jason?'

He could hardly tell her the truth. He didn't know her well enough to explain that Hanna Silverstein appeared to want him for his body rather than his acting talent.

'It's just that she's being very cagey about the script. And she won't tell me anything about the sort of part it is, or the screen test.'

'Give her time. She's a busy woman.'

'It's just . . .'

'Just what? Jason, they've spent a lot of money getting you out there, haven't they? First class travel. It was first class, wasn't it?'

'Oh yes.'

'Accommodation . . .'

'Clothes . . .'

'Clothes?'

'She's bought me clothes. Insisted. There wasn't time to pack anything.'

'Well, there you are. What are you worried about? They wouldn't spend that sort of money if they weren't serious, would they? It wouldn't make any sense.'

'Suppose not.'

'You got a pen?'

'Yes.'

'Take this number down: 743 8080. George Hammerstein. He's our associate on the coast. Lovely man. Go and see him tomorrow. I'll ring him and fix it up. Any problems, talk to him. He knows everyone out there.'

'Hammerstein?'

'That's it. He's a top agent. Got some of the biggest stars on his books. And don't worry.'

'OK.'

'Jason, I know a thousand actors who'd give their right arm to be doing what you're doing. Just lie back and enjoy it.'

'You're right.'

'I'm always right.'

They exchanged goodbyes. Jason felt better, much better.


Hanna hadn't been home when he got back from Martha's house

and Maria had told him she wasn't expected back until late.

His rehearsed and re-rehearsed showdown had therefore had to be postponed and he'd decided to ring Joy Chivas instead. What she'd said made a great deal of sense. He decided to accept her advice, though he hoped she would never realise quite how literally. He would lie back and enjoy it. Why not? As Joy said, Hanna had spent a lot of money on him. She was a smart businesswoman. She'd hardly bring him all the way from London just to be her stud. Los Angeles was full of actors who could fulfil that role at little or no expense.

Hanna had a drink problem. She was moody and subject to wild swings of emotion. From the almost girl-like creature he had seen by the pool this morning she had turned into a rude, foul-mouthed harridan. What mood she would be in when she got home tonight and how sober she'd be, he had no way of knowing but clearly he had to accept that she was going to talk about his professional duties when she was good and ready, and not one moment before.

Maria cooked him a delicious meal of meatloaf and baked potatoes with pecan pie and whipped cream. He ate voraciously, much to Maria's delight. She doled out second helpings, her pleasant chubby face creased in a smile that was reflected in her soft brown eyes.

'Ms Hanna, she never eats. I like to cook.'

'It was great.'

'American food.'

'Are you from Mexico?'

'*Si*. Half the population of Los Angeles is from Mexico . . .' she laughed. 'Without us the city would stop.'

The food made him tired. He went up to bed with one of the

books he had brought with him, after trying to watch American television and finding the numerous commercial breaks too much to bear.

Before he realised it had happened he was asleep, a deep, dreamless sleep, the balmy night air carried in through the open window.

It was the light that woke him, daylight, the first light of dawn filtering through the drawn curtains. He sat up, feeling totally refreshed. The bed besides him was empty but from the state of it Hanna had clearly slept next to him. The book he had been reading was now on the bedside table.

He climbed into a towelling robe and went downstairs, knowing, this time, where Hanna would be. Sure enough outside in the pool Hanna Silverstein was powering apparently effortlessly up and down with the same elegant stroke, her body, like a fish, hardly disturbing the water at all. Jason poured himself an orange juice from the fridge and sat watching her again, hoping her mood would also be the same as it had been yesterday morning.

Eventually she pulled herself up from the edge of the pool.

'Morning,' she said.

'Morning. Good swim?'

'Wonderful.'

She took his glass of orange juice and sipped it, then sat herself astride his lap. This morning her one-piece swimsuit was white. White complimented her tan as much as black.

'You were so fast asleep when I came in I couldn't bear to wake you.' She smiled, stroking his cheek with her hand.

'Jet lag.'

'I get it more in London than I do here.'

'I don't think I'd ever get tired of watching you swim.'

'Really? I love it. I forget everything, you know, the water just washes over me, it feels so cool, so smooth. I think I must have been a fish in a previous life.'

'You swim like a ballet dancer. So graceful.'

'That's a lovely thing to say.'

She looked about twenty-five, her wet hair clinging to her head, her wrinkles smoothed away by her relaxation. She stroked his cheek with the back of her hand.

'I'm sorry,' she said.

'For what?'

'For being so bloody-minded most of the time. It's the job. This town . . . everything. It gets to me. You wouldn't believe the pressure. It's constant. You'd think after all the films I've made people would actually trust me. Instead of which I have to go begging for money like I've never made a film before . . .'

He could actually see lines breaking out on her face as the thought of work broke through the calm created by the swimming.

'I understand,' he said.

'You're very sweet.'

'It must be tough.'

'No. I don't want to think about that yet,' she said decisively. 'Not quite yet.' But the lines were etched into her face and did not go away. 'Come over here, there's something I want to show you.'

The Californian sun reflected off the swimming pool making it glimmer like liquid silver. At this time in the morning the cicadas hadn't begun their continuous beat and everything was quiet.

Hanna took his hand and led him over to the side of the house. Here, tacked on like an afterthought to the main building, another room had been built overlooking the gardens. Hanna took a key from under a flower pot outside the room's only door and let them in. The room was dark, the windows veiled with heavy curtains. Hanna pressed a button on a small control panel and electric motors whirred them apart to reveal two large picture windows with panoramic views of the huge gardens.

'This is where I come to get away from it all. There's no door into the main house, no telephone, no fax,' she said, adding more pointedly, 'and no booze.'

The room was very feminine in decor, Jason thought. There were none of the memorabilia of the film business that were scattered throughout the main house, not a poster or a prop in sight. No scripts, either. Nothing to do with the film business at all. Mounted in pride of place on the wall above one of the chintz sofas was a small Renoir. Could it be a real Renoir?

On one of the small occasional tables there were pictures of an elderly woman arm in arm with Hanna and another woman of a similar age.

Hanna saw him looking. 'My mother and sister,' she explained.

'She's pretty.'

'I never bring anyone in here.'

'It's so different from the rest of the house.'

'I suppose so.'

Hanna stripped off the shoulder straps of the white swimsuit and pulled it down off her thin body. She dabbed herself dry with the towel she had brought.

'Jason . . . I need you. I mean badly. For comfort.'

She came over to him and put her arms around his body, hugging herself to him with tears welling in her eyes. He hugged her too.

'Love me . . .' she whispered.

She untied the belt of the robe and insinuated her hands under it to hug his naked back, pressing her body into him. He felt his erection grow.

She dropped to her knees and gobbled his cock into her mouth, sucking more blood up into the shaft. As soon as it was fully erect Hanna got to her feet again. Taking Jason's hand she led him over to one of the large chintz-covered sofas. She lay on her back.

'Love me baby . . .' she said, her eyes still full of tears.

He sat on the edge of the sofa and trailed his hand down her neck. He was about to caress her breasts.

'No.'

She pulled him down on to her body, opened her legs and used her hand to guide his cock to the lips of her cunt. She was dry. He started to move his hand down to her sex in an attempt to make her wet.

'No,' she said again. 'Just do it. Force it . . .'

He felt her hand holding his cock against the mouth of her sex and did as she asked. He pushed against the dry unyielding flesh, feeling her wispy pubic hair like wire wool against the head of his cock.

'Yes . . .' she encouraged. 'Oh yes.'

He pushed again. This time he penetrated not more than an inch. Beyond that the way was barred, the opening sealed up. He pushed again, urged on by her hands which had moved round to his bare rump under the robe. Another thrust and he felt a slickness, a hint of wetness. Suddenly, dramatically, the hint turned into a flood and his cock rode all the way into her cunt.

'Yes . . .' she said triumphantly.

There was something exciting about feeling her body give way over him like this, desire explicitly presented, something that made his cock harden even more, something that he knew he would not be able to control.

Hanna was liquid now, squirming under him, the tears in her eyes replaced by need. She pulled the white towelling robe off his shoulders and threw it aside. She thrust her hips up off the sofa to meet his thrusts. She was moaning very quietly.

Jason was coming and he couldn't control it. He didn't know why. He was usually able to endure much more than this. But Hanna felt so soft, so feminine, her need so different from what she had been like before, emotional need rather than sexual and for some perverse reason that was making him come.

She could feel it. She could feel him trying to hold himself back.

'Don't,' she whispered in his ear. 'Come. Let it come. I want it . . .' She pushed her tongue into the curls of his ear.

And he did. Her tongue was the last straw. He had slowed his thrusts to try and hold on longer but now, at her bidding, with her fingers digging into his buttocks, again pushing them forward, he resumed his tempo, pushing the head of his cock right up inside her where it was exposed to all those delicious feelings, where her hot wet cunt clung to it, sucked at it, devoured it.

He felt his cock pulsing and at the same time Hanna's cunt

seemed to contract around it. They were coming together, their needs equal, their fulfilment matched.

'God . . .' she managed to moan.

As his spunk powered out of his cock, the walls of her cunt contracted with the same rhythm, opening as it spurted, closing and clinging and close as it relaxed. Their bodies locked together, their eyes closed together, their nerves exploded together. They were out of control, the orgasm of one stoking the fires of the other. It seemed to go on forever. It drove them both high, out of themselves, out of everything but the feeling of indescribable sensation.

They came down slowly, floating down like a feather drifting on the wind, occasionally taken higher again by some thermal current, before eventually falling to earth. The little tremors and shocks in the aftermath of orgasm took them higher before eventually their bodies released them from the need for pleasure.

Jason rolled off Hanna's body. If he hadn't been able to feel her response he would have apologised for being so quick. It was not like him. As it was he didn't think he had anything to apologise for.

'Oh God . . .' she said. 'Don't want to come down.'

'Don't, then.'

The sun was shining through the big windows. Curiously, in the harsh daylight Hanna's face looked young again, as it had by the side of the pool.

'I have to.'

Outside the pool man had arrived and was starting to drag the water with a long tube attached to a cylindrical vacuum cleaner.

Hanna got up off the sofa and wrapped the towel around her thin body.

'I need a drink,' she said in an entirely different tone of voice.

And Jason knew what that meant.

# Chapter Five

Hanna had encouraged Jason to use any of the cars in the garage and it had taken him some time to decide between the Ferrari and the Mercedes. Eventually he had chosen the Mercedes since it would probably be easier to drive in an unfamiliar city. The Ferrari would be a handful, would provide an irresistible temptation to speed, and having an accident in it would definitely not be a good idea, bearing in mind his current position in the Silverstein hierarchy.

He found a street map in the glove compartment and worked out how to get to George Hammerstein's office on Sunset Boulevard. It looked easy. And it was. The Boulevards of Los Angeles ran the whole length of the city. It was only a question of finding the number on the building. Nor was that a problem. Most of the office and apartment blocks, he had noticed, had their numbers emblazoned in ten-foot letters mounted on their roof tops.

The car, an automatic, responded to his commands effortlessly. Its silky smoothness reminded him of the way Hanna had responded to him this morning, the minimum of effort for the maximum result. The gearbox changed so quietly it was almost impossible to feel it happening, the engine delivering power without the slightest hint of friction.

As soon as he had found his way north from Santa Monica Boulevard up to Sunset he saw the building he was heading for. The huge black letters announcing 9000 SUNSET could be seen from at least two miles away on the top of a six-storey office block.

Parking was easy too. The restaurants all had valet parking as did the shops. The office and apartment buildings each had their own parking lot either in the basement or alongside, and 9000 Sunset had parking in the building on the ground floor. Jason was handed a parking ticket as he drove in.

Carefully locking the car he took the lift to the fifth floor. His lunch date, arranged by phone his morning, was for 12.30 p.m. and it was just 12.15.

'Mr Hammerstein,' he said to the girl on the reception desk outside the lift, under a big silver sign with lettering etched into the metal: HAMMERSTEIN AND COHEN.

'Is he expecting you?' the blonde receptionist said, her eyes obviously appreciating Jason's physique.

'Jason MacIver.'

'That's an unusual name.'

'Scottish originally.'

'Really? Actually, I think Mr Hammerstein's out at lunch. Hold on . . .' She punched two buttons on the small switchboard console on her desk. 'Nancy. Jason's here,' she said, then turned back to him. 'Can I validate you?'

'Sorry?'

'Validate?'

'I don't understand.'

'Validate your parking ticket. Otherwise you have to pay.'

'Oh. Thanks.' He found the ticket and handed it over. She

stamped it with an office stamp and handed it back to him.

The receptionist was slim and attractive. Just as he was wondering why every girl he had seen in Los Angeles seemed to be from the same gene pool of beauty another example swung through the double doors that led to the main offices.

'Hi!'

The girl was a tall brunette. She wore a tight-fitting and very short dark green dress. Her long legs were encased in a sort of translucent, shimmery, white nylon. Though the neckline of the dress clung to her throat and did not reveal any cleavage, her bust projected almost at right angles, a deep firm pillow of pulchritude. Making no concessions to her height she wore spiky high heels in green suede.

'Nancy Dockery. I'm George's assistant,' she said, extending her hand to be shaken. Her eyes were the deepest brown, her black hair obviously long, but pinned up in a complex plait at the back of her head. 'And you're Jason MacIver. Come through.'

Jason shook her hand. It was cool to the touch. He followed her buoyant hips through the double doors as she lead the way across a large open plan office where six or seven secretaries worked behind their desks. Everywhere, on every wall space, were posters of films and framed cuttings of film reviews. On every desk was a pile of film scripts each with its title printed in felt pen on the binding. Along the outside of this space were individual offices partitioned by very thin walls. Nancy piloted him into one of these, its outer wall a plate of glass from floor to ceiling, the view of the huge flat sprawl of Los Angeles spectacular from this height.

'If I worked in here I think I'd spend all day staring out of the window,' Jason said, standing and staring.

'Listen, I'm afraid George has had to go out. There's a problem at Warner Bros. Script changes one of our clients doesn't like. The usual thing . . . It was really urgent.'

The disappointment showed on Jason's face.

'He was really looking forward to meeting you. Sit, please . . .'

Jason sat in one of the two leather wing chairs in front of the desk. Nancy sat in the other. On the desk there was a large silver-framed photograph of a man and a woman holding two children around the shoulders. Presumably this was the missing George Hammerstein.

'I really wanted to see him about Hanna Silverstein.'

'Yes. Joy Chivas phoned. She thinks you're a real comer . . .'

'Did she explain the problem?'

'Problem?'

'Yes.'

'She said you had a screen test for Hanna Silverstein's next picture.'

'Exactly, that's what I wanted to talk to George about.'

'Is there a problem?' Nancy's dark brown eyes seemed to express real concern. She had crossed her long legs. The muscles on the top of her thigh looked as though they had been perfectly sculpted from some anatomical textbook.

'Yes. Well, don't know. I think so. I would just like him to ask her if I can see a script or at least find out what the part is. I don't even know what the film is called.'

'*The Casting Couch.*'

'What?'

'*The Casting Couch.* That's what the film is called. It's a modern sex comedy with a thriller element. Well, that's what the studios put out . . .'

'Well, that's the first I've heard. You see, if he could at least find out when the screen test is going to be . . .'

'She's not said anything?'

'Not since . . . It's difficult for me . . .'

'Difficult?'

'Yes. Let's just say she seems to want to have more than just a professional relationship.'

'What else is new?'

'Sorry?'

'Jason, this may be a shock to you but you're not the first. Hanna has a reputation in this town. She has a . . . penchant . . . for young actors . . .'

'What does that mean?'

'It means nothing.'

'Does it mean she's not going to test me?'

'No. No, not at all.' Nancy tried to sound reassuring.

'Well, that's why I need help. That's what agents are for, isn't it?'

'Right.'

'Can George call her, then? Just establish when the test's going to be. I mean, I've got no complaints. I'm living in the lap of luxury. I just want to know the situation.'

'Right. I'll explain it to him. I'm sure he'll call her.'

'Great.'

'Jason . . .' Nancy uncrossed her legs. The miniscule skirt of the dress had ridden up even more on the leather chair and Jason could see a triangle of the crotch of her apparently black knickers under the shimmery tights. He could even see wisps of pubic hair escaping from underneath the material, crushed by the nylon. He hoped she had not seen him staring. She was looking at him seriously, those brown eyes unwavering. 'Can I give you a bit of private advice?'

'I'd appreciate it.'

'Hanna Silverstein is a big name in Hollywood. She's got a big reputation. A lot of people in this town are afraid of her. She's got a lot of friends, too.'

'And?'

'And, don't get on the wrong side of her, that's all.'

'I met Martha Morris yesterday.'

'Oh?'

'She told me Hanna was into porn films.'

Nancy didn't look shocked. 'Hollywood needs the money, Jason. It's a big business. Very big business.'

'But I thought . . .'

'There's an expression here, whatever runs, runs.'

'Well, I know there's a lot of it around . . .'

'Listen, George said to take you out to lunch. There's a little place across the road . . .'

'That would be nice.'

'Come on then. We can walk.'

They walked across the street to a restaurant that was designed to look like a set from a cowboy film, with sawdust on the floor and wooden beams across the ceiling. Seated at a round table. with a blue gingham tablecloth Jason was relieved when Nancy ordered wine. He needed a drink. What she had told him had hardly improved his mood. He was equally glad that she seemed prepared to join him in eating a hamburger and fries, not opting for the house salad that was so prominent on the menu. Once again Jason was starving.

They talked incessantly but Hanna Silverstein was not mentioned again. Nancy's mind seemed alert and wide-ranging. She wanted to talk about books and English politics and international diplomacy. She was keen to hear about Jason's history and training at RADA and compare it with the American system.

After two hours of constant talk and their third refill of coffee Nancy looked at her watch.

'I'd better get back,' she said.

She paid the bill and walked Jason back to the Mercedes.

'Thanks,' he said. 'That was the most normal conversation I've had since I've been here.'

'Oh, don't get the wrong idea. I can be as abnormal as the rest of them.' There was a sparkle in her eyes as she said it, suggesting Jason had no idea what.

'Well, that's an avenue I'd like to explore . . .'

'Good.' She rummaged in her handbag and eventually found a little notebook with a propelling pencil attached. She scribbled in it and tore off the result. 'Home telephone. If you fancy escaping from the heights of Beverly Hills and slumming it in Westwood, give me a ring.'

'I'd like that a lot, Nancy.'

'I'd like that a lot too, Jason. I think I could surprise you . . .'

With that she kissed him on the cheek, and turned to walk to the lift. He watched her go, the high heels shaping her calves and tilting her full arse into a pout. He felt his cock twitch.

'Down, boy,' he said to himself as he got into the car. He drove out of the car park, handed the attendant his validated ticket and turned left back up to Beverly Hills.

Hanna emerged from the dressing room with the bourbon glass in her hand.

'Jason,' she barked.

Jason was standing by the front windows watching the big stretch Cadillac limousine manoeuvring up to the front door.

'Can you just get this hook . . .'

The dress Hanna was wearing looked, from a distance, as if it were made of gold chain-mail. Actually it was made from a type of silk spun and woven to resemble exactly the texture of metal but with none of its weight. It shimmered in the light, its shape a plain shift, the material dramatic enough not to need further elaboration. There was a small hook at the back that secured the neckline.

Jason came over and slotted the hook through the corresponding eye with no difficulty. Hanna's hairdresser had visited her at the house in the late afternoon and her hair was curled into soft flattering waves.

'You look great,' Jason said, and meant it.

'Sure,' she said, obviously not in the mood for compliments. 'That Armani looks good on you.'

He was wearing the darkest of the two suits they had bought with a black shirt and black tie. Dark was in, Hanna had told him.

Then minutes later they were in the back of the Cadillac in the stream of traffic on a five-lane freeway heading for Burbank Studios.

'Get me a bourbon,' Hanna said.

'Do you think . . .'

'Jason,' her voice was edged with steel, 'never say what you were about to say. Never.'

'None of my business. Sorry.'

'You got that right.'

He reached into the custom-made cocktail cabinet and poured her a glass of Jim Beam, knowing by now not to bother trying to make it a small one.

Despite this rebuke Jason was in a surprisingly good mood. At first what Nancy had told him about Hanna had depressed him but when he looked back on what had happened this morning, how she'd allowed him to share a real intimacy, he felt they had established a base for mutual respect and understanding, however she treated him the rest of the day. That was just a function of her wild and erratic changes of mood. In a sense he was comforted by the news that he was not the first actor to come under Ms Silverstein's spell. That would make things a great deal easier when the time came to assert his professional status as an actor and sever the personal relationship.

George Hammerstein would sort it all out. He didn't have to worry about bringing the subject up himself. No more speeches to rehearse. It was a weight off his shoulders. That was what agents were for.

Hopefully, if the screen test was successful – and he would make sure it was – and a contract was signed it would not be too long before professional needs took precedence. It couldn't be too soon for him. He didn't want to have to put up with Hanna's moods any longer than he had to.

On top of all that they were on their way to a studio. For the first time he was actually going to see the back lot of a

Hollywood studio even if it was only to go to a 'wrap' party to celebrate the completion of the studio's latest product. There were bound to be other actors there, fellow professionals. It would make him feel like he belonged, someone there in his own right, not just an appendage of Hanna Silverstein.

The Cadillac slowed as they turned into the studio gates. Security guards checked the occupants of a line of expensive cars, many of them stretch Cadillacs.

'Evening, Ms Silverstein,' the gate guard said.

'Evening, Freddie,' Hanna replied, waving the bourbon glass at him.

They were waved through. The car headed down the road between the massive walls of the sound stages. Ahead Jason could see an area of really bright light. The Cadillac stopped and the chauffeur opened the passenger door. Hanna climbed out without a word. Jason followed.

In the light of a hundred spotlights a section of New York street was illuminated, brownstone tenements complete with front steps and trash cans, the road running down the middle of the set, parked with fifties cars, every detail perfect. There were sidewalks with curbstones – made of plaster – and hydrants and lamp posts and a hot dog stand all designed to fit the period.

In the middle of the street trestle tables had been set up laden with food and drink. Waitresses dressed in body stockings made from red fish net with little red satin inserts covering – or at least attempting to cover – their nipples and pubic triangles, plied the guests with glasses of champagne.

Jason lost sight of Hanna immediately. She had made a bee-line for one of the tables and after she'd got a large bourbon from a waitress whose satin panels could not contain a mammoth pair of breasts ('I know the doctor who gave them to her,' Hanna told him) she was taken off by a small, fat, bald man who appeared to want to talk to her urgently about something.

Left to wander Jason examined the street to find it was only a series of 'flats' held up at the back by scaffolding and metal supports. One or two of the endless succession of attractive women, the majority of whom seemed to have been cloned from the same genes – long blonde hair, big breasts, small bums and long legs – approached him but as he definitely did not want to become attached and have Hanna discover him with some young cutey, he talked to them politely then made his excuses. None of them, in any event, were actresses, though they all said they wanted to be.

He did find one actor, a big black man who looked as if he had once taken weight training very seriously but whose physique had since gone rapidly downhill. He, however, was more interested in finding a supply of cocaine than talking to Jason about the role he had just completed.

It was fascinating to see the scale and lavishness of the real Hollywood. Champagne flowed, cameras flashed, a rock band played loudly at one end of the set, and a huge cake in the shape of a fifties Buick was presented to the film's stars, an unshaven actor who Jason had first seen in a television series (and whose involvement in this picture had reportedly cost the studio five million dollars) and a blonde, big-breasted leading lady of about twenty-five.

The cake, cut and distributed by the scantily clad waitresses – all no doubt, waiting for their chance at fame and fortune –

tasted revolting, the icing apparently designed to keep Hollywood's legions of dentists in work for months to come.

'Jason.' Hanna's hand goosed Jason's arse so hard he cried out in pain, spinning round to assault the perpetrator. Hanna stood with the small, fat, bald, man and a statuesque blonde in a red dress that looked as though it had been sprayed on to her body, it fitted so tightly.

'Jason MacIver. This is Bill Talbot and Mrs Talbot.'

'Pleased to meet you,' Jason said, beaming. He shook Bill's hand first and then his wife's. The latter held out her hand but did not move it at all. It was like shaking hands with a limp fish.

'I've told them all about you, Jason. Bill is the head of the studio here.'

Well that's more like it, Jason thought. Now we're getting somewhere. He smiled eagerly. Bill Talbot smiled back, Mrs Talbot did not, giving the impression that she was tremendously bored. The dress was backless. At the front the neckline of the clinging material was so deep it finished at the waist. The silk revealed the shape of her heavy pendulant breasts, outlining every curve. The skirt of the dress followed the line of her perfect apple of an arse just as accurately. It was full length and tight right down to her ankles, allowing her to walk only in tiny steps. If she was wearing knickers they would have had to be made from gossamer, Jason thought. Anything else would have shown under the creaseless dress. Her blonde hair was cut in a fashionable bob.

'I like English actors. Real class,' Talbot said.

'Well, there are a lot of us,' Jason replied, pleased to include himself in the 'us'.

'And most of them over here,' Hanna added.

'That's for sure,' Talbot laughed. 'Listen, Hanna, I've had a pig of a day. We're going home.'

'Sure, you go. I'll call you tomorrow.'

'I'll give him points out of ten.'

'You call me then.'

What this exchange meant Jason did not know except it was obviously referring to him.

'Thanks again. He looks great.' As he was clearly talking about him Jason felt another jolt of encouragement. 'Our car's over here . . .' Talbot said to him.

'Your car?'

'Bill's asked you back to his house for a drink, Jason,' Hanna said quickly.

'That's very nice.'

Hanna pulled his sleeve so he bent to listen to her whisper, 'He wants to get to know you . . .'

'Great.'

'Come on, then,' Talbot said with the air of someone whose patience was not inexhaustible.

'It's very nice of you to . . . ah . . .'

'Any friend of Hanna's is a friend of ours. Right?' He laughed heartily at this and took Jason's arm.

'See you later,' Hanna said, waving.

'Aren't you coming?' It had not occurred to him that he was meant to go alone.

'See you back at the house.' And before Jason could protest Hanna had disappeared into the crowd.

Talbot guided Jason along the New York street, their progress slowed by Mrs Talbot's tiny steps. A Rolls Royce stood at the end of the set. It was no ordinary Rolls Royce. This was a stretch version. A chauffeur stood with the rear doors open. Mrs Talbot climbed into the car through the nearest, while Talbot went round to the far side. Jason waited, as Mrs Talbot adjusted the dress to enable her to sit down without ripping it, then got in after her. There was a pull-up bucket seat in the large passenger compartment. Jason sat in it facing the Talbots. He tried to relax. This was obviously going to be important for his career. Bill Talbot was an important man, probably the most important.

So far Mrs Talbot had not said a word. She had looked at him, though, and he was aware of her eyes on him now. Their interest appeared more than casual. For half a second their eyes met. Hers were a marine blue. He looked away. The last thing he needed was the sexual attention of the studio head's wife.

'So you're doing Hanna's next picture,' he said, as the car pulled away almost silently.

'Sure.' Talbot was looking at him, his eyes flicking up and down his body.

'When do you think it'll start?'

'Start?'

'Start shooting.'

'Does it matter?' His tone of annoyance was obvious.

'Suppose not.' Jason thought better of pursuing that line of conversation.

'She's promised to test you, right?'

'She brought me over from London.'

'Typical,' Talbot said. 'More money than sense.'

'I think she wanted an English actor for the part.'

'Yah, yah . . .' His voice was deep and gruff. He was the

108

sort of man that made Jason feel callow and inexperienced. Jason had no idea what to say next.

'Are you pleased with the new film?'

'What new film?'

'The wrap party . . .'

'Oh that. Do we have to talk business, kid?'

'Sorry.' Things were not going well. He decided to shut up and let Talbot make the conversation.

He did just that. 'What do you think of my wife?' he said, as though asking Jason if he liked some painting.

'She's very beautiful.' It was his turn to talk about someone as though they didn't exist.

'Do you fancy her?'

What sort of question was that? Jason thought in alarm.

'She's very attractive,' he said guardedly.

'Good.'

There was a silence. Mrs Talbot was looking at Jason again. He suddenly had the feeling that something was very wrong.

'You can touch,' Talbot said as the big car started climbing up into the Hollywood Hills.

'Sorry?'

'You can touch her.'

'I don't understand . . .'

'I mean touch her . . . before we get home.'

'Touch her?'

'Touch her. Feel her. You speak English?'

'Why should I touch her?'

Talbot guffawed with laughter. His wife looked out of the car window.

'That's what you're here for.'

'What!'

'Christ, didn't Hanna tell you?'

'Tell me what?'

'Look, pretty boy. We're going to my home. You're going to fuck my wife. I watch. Is that simple enough for you? Words of one syllable. Christ, I expected Hanna to explain all this. I shouldn't have to do this.'

'She didn't . . .'

'So that's it. You got it. That's the deal.' Talbot's voice was angry.

'I don't . . .'

'I hope you aren't going to say what I think you're going to say, kid. Because if you are you're getting out of this car now and I'm calling Hanna on that phone and telling her there's going to be no damn screen test for no damn English actor. You got it?'

'Yes.'

'So what were you going to say?' Talbot leant forward in his seat.

'Nothing.'

'That's better.' Talbot slumped back.

Jason's mind was spinning. Hanna had used him, bartered him away in return for what he did not know. He ground his teeth. His worst suspicions were rapidly being fulfilled. What was he supposed to do now? If he refused that would be the end of that. No screen test. He couldn't see Hanna Silverstein supporting him against Talbot. His only comfort was that Talbot appeared to know all about the screen test. At least Hanna hadn't lied about that.

And there was another consolation. Mrs Talbot was a very beautiful woman.

He realised that the divider between the driver and the passengers was still lowered. Talbot appeared perfectly content for his chauffeur to hear this conversation.

'So . . .' Talbot said.

Jason looked blank.

'Touch her. Take a tit out of her dress. Feel it. Play with it.'

Jason could hardly believe what he was hearing.

'Come on . . .' Talbot said in the tone of voice he would use at a meeting where an executive was taking too long to get to the point.

Jason leaned forward but could not reach without getting up from the seat. He got down on his knees in front of the red dress. Mrs Talbot turned her blue eyes to look at him in the light of the passing street lamps.

This was the strangest experience of his life, Jason thought, as he reached out his hand and cupped her heavy breast in his palm. Her nipple was hard. He pulled the silky material aside and in the lights that flashed by, saw her big ovoid tit. The aureola of her breast was a thick dark brown, her nipple large and prominent.

Bill Talbot had moved into the corner of the seat, twisting round and bringing one leg up on to the leather so he could see without turning his head.

'She's a bitch . . .' he breathed so quietly it was only just audible. 'Aren't you?' he said more loudly.

'Yes,' she said, the first word she'd spoken. Her accent sounded almost English.

'Come on . . .' Talbot urged.

Jason weighed the breast in his hand, played with the hard nipple, not at all sure what he should do. Talbot lent forward so his face was inches from his wife's.

'She's a bitch. What do you do with bitches? Make her moan . . .'

He rocked back into the corner of the seat again. He could see the chauffeur watching in the rearview mirror.

Jason pinched the hard nipple. Nothing happened. He pinched it harder. Mrs Talbot let out a dull moan that had nothing to do with pain.

They were passing through the gates of a huge mansion, which closed electrically behind them. The car swept up a steep driveway to a vast house. Its gothic design made it look like the set for a horror film set in Victorian England.

The chauffeur parked the car opposite the front door. He opened the nearest passenger door of the Rolls which happened to be the door on Talbot's side. The small, fat, bald man got out and went to open the front door. Mrs Talbot followed, making no attempt to cover her breast. Jason climbed out last. As he looked around, the chauffeur, a big burly black man, took his arm.

'Bud,' he whispered, 'don't sweat it. This is all a game. Got it? She's into it as much as he is. You dig?'

'I don't understand any of it.'

'Then you better learn fast if you want to get on.' The chauffeur winked conspiratorially, released Jason's arm and got back into the Rolls. He was athletic looking and young. Why didn't they use him? Jason thought. Or perhaps they already had.

As the Rolls pulled away in a crunch of gravel and with about as much enthusiasm as a fly knowingly stepping into a spider's web, Jason walked through the ornate front door. The interior of the house did not match the exterior at all. Inside everything was totally modern, steel and chrome and leather and fine veneered furniture, chairs made of plate glass, rugs woven in copies of Mondrian paintings, and, on the walls, a collection of modern art to rival Martha Morris's.

The main hall was dominated by a long stainless steel staircase with balustrades fashioned from steel cables. It curved round to an open landing on the first floor.

Mrs Talbot hitched her skirt up slightly to enable her to climb the steps. She was wearing red high heels. They clattered nosily on the steel.

Talbot had gone to a black lacquered cabinet which held the booze and poured two large cognacs from a bottle of Hine Antique into two large balloon glasses. He drank his down in one gulp and handed the other to Jason. 'Hanna should have told you, kid. She should have told you.'

'She's got a lot on her mind.' Why he was apologising for Hanna he couldn't imagine. No, that was wrong. He knew why. He didn't want Talbot to be annoyed with Hanna in case it affected the film.

Jason sipped the brandy. He needed it. He followed Talbot up the staircase, their shoes clanging on the steel.

The bedroom contained only two bedside tables on either side of a large double bed. The bed was placed in the middle of the room, not against one wall. The bed was covered with a single black sheet. In the middle of the bed lay a shining object. The light in the room was dim and it was not until he got closer that Jason saw the object was in fact a dildo, a huge phallus fashioned in what he was sure was silver. It was the work of a craftsman, every detail of an erect penis, the slit of the urethra, the acorn shape of the glans, the thick bulbous tube on the outer surface, the veins and gnarls of tumescence, all reproduced perfectly. Had it not been in shining metal it would have looked real. The base was flared. The craftsman had not bothered to fashion a scrotum or balls; that had not been required.

Mrs Talbot unfastened the dress at the back of her neck and let its halter fall to her waist. It fell no further. She had to shimmy her way out of the skirt. She was naked underneath as Jason had suspected; no tights, no panties. Her pubic hair was blonde, fine and sparse. He could see the first inch of the crease of her sex. Her heavy breasts trembled, pendulums of flesh.

Perhaps it was Jason's imagination but he thought he saw a look pass between husband and wife, a look of compliance, a look of anticipation. He saw the slightest of smiles flicker over her lips before her face became virtually expressionless again. Or did he?

She lay on the bed, moving the dildo to one side, lying on her stomach in the middle of the black sheet with her legs wide open. Her buttocks were ripe and long, swelling out from the small of her back in the shape of a succulent plum.

Jason could see her labia, like the mouth of some exotic fruit, fringed by her wispy fine pubic hair. He could see the corona of her anus, at the top of her sex, an inverted exclamation mark. The cleft between her legs was unusually wide, unusually flat, the width of a hand almost. Her big breasts, squashed under her weight, ballooned out at either side of her chest.

It had a ritual quality. Her position defined by time. Was Jason the sacrifice or the priest? Almost despite himself his cock hardened.

So fascinated had Jason been by his wife, he had not realised that Talbot had left the room, until he saw him coming back. He was naked apart from a towel wrapped around his fat belly. He put a tube of KY-Jelly next to the dildo.

'You bitch,' he said. He sat on the edge of the bed by his wife's head.

'I'm not a bitch,' she said. Her accent was from New England, clear, crisp vowel sounds in stark contrast to Talbot's drawling New York Bronx.

'You're a bitch. You're always screwing other men. Eyeing them up. You bitch.'

'Fuck off,' she said, the words sounding strange out of her cultured mouth.

'Do you want to be tied?'

'No.'

'You know what you're going to do?' Talbot said to Jason.

'You better tell me.'

'Fuck her. Hard.'

Jason understood that. He stripped off his Armani suit and the black shirt. His cock bobbed into view, glad to be freed from the prison of his trousers.

'One day I'm going to have you gangbanged. That's what you deserve. A slut like you. A slut like you. Tits hanging out, arse hanging out, just begging for it. That's what you deserve.' It was all part of the ritual, ritual abuse, ritual foreplay.

'No . . .' she said, but from the tone of her voice it was impossible to believe the idea didn't excite her.

'You slut . . .'

Jason knelt between her open legs, his erection standing

almost vertical. Talbot picked up the dildo and handed it to him.

'In her arse,' he hissed.

'No,' she said immediately, but again the tone sounded as if she were saying 'yes'.

The dildo was cold to the touch. Jason felt as though he were in some sort of dream, like an elaborate wet dream, except it had a nightmare quality. He seemed to have no will of his own. He just did as he was told. He lubricated the shaft of the dildo then spurted the gel around her anus. As he did she seemed to arch it back at him in invitation. Her anus seemed to be winking at him, the mouth of her sex under it squirming too, squirming with need.

He looked up at Talbot as though snapping out of a trance.

'Do it,' Talbot mouthed.

Jason placed the head of the silver cock at her anus and felt her tremble. He pushed it forward gently and to his total surprise it disappeared into her body as though he had thrust it in with all his might. Obviously she'd relaxed, waiting for it, wanting it. And now she had it, now it was buried inside her, her whole body convulsed in front of his eyes, writhing on the black sheet as it struggled to express her instant orgasm.

Talbot watched. 'You slut,' he said quietly. 'See what she's like.'

'I am . . .' she said, her voice breathy with passion. 'I want everything, I want to fuck everything.'

The flared base of the dildo seemed to have been tailored to the width of her crotch it fitted so well against the cheeks of her arse.

'Fuck her,' Talbot said.

'No, no,' she cried.

Jason lowered himself on to her beautiful, sleek body. His cock felt the coldness of the silver. He dipped it lower and, by contrast, suddenly felt the heat and wetness of her cunt. He thrust himself forward. It was an extraordinary sensation. One side of her cunt was rigid and cold, the silver hardly warmed at all by her body heat, the other pliant and hot and wet.

He raised himself on his arms and looked down at her long slim back and the mound of her arse. He looked over at Talbot who had taken off the towel and was masturbating himself while his little piggy eyes watched the proceedings.

Under him he felt the woman's body quiver. He could feel her cunt pulsing and knew she was coming again.

'Two cocks . . .' she moaned quietly. She reared up from the bed, arching her back like a bow, bringing her head back until it touched Jason's face, as far back as it would go, like a feat of gymnastics. Her cunt squeezed on his cock and she moaned, keeping her back bent, supporting herself on her arms, until the quivering stopped and she sunk back on the bed, the crisis of orgasm passed.

'You bastard,' she muttered in the same tone as if she were saying, 'I love you.'

Quickly and with a lot of strength, she rolled over on to her side taking Jason with her, his cock held firm inside her.

'Not enough,' she said. She was facing towards her husband.

'Not enough,' Talbot said to Jason, his fist still pummelling his cock.

What did they want him to do? He thrust harder.

'Take it out,' she ordered. He wasn't sure whether she meant his cock or the silver dildo. He would have been delighted to take the dildo out. Its presence made her cunt inhospitable. The flared base was digging uncomfortably into the bottom of his cock.

To get the dildo out he would have to withdraw his cock. He pulled out of her then began to pull the dildo out too. She rolled back on to her stomach.

'Slowly . . . do it very slowly,' she ordered.

As he obeyed he could see the thick oval of her labia pulsing, the whole of her sex glistening with juices. He pulled the crafted silver dildo out of her anus as slowly as he could and watched as her body worked itself to orgasm. She had done this before. Many times before. She had trained herself to come at the last moment, as the silver phallus finally left her.

'Now . . .' she said, her whole body tensed. He pulled the dildo clear. She came, her body convulsing, arching off the bed and flopping back again, her muscles locked in a spasm of pleasure.

Jason had been so involved in watching her he hadn't noticed Talbot. Presumably he'd come too. He was using the towel to wipe his hand. He got up off the bed.

'I'm going to go to bed now,' he said, the tone of his voice completely different. All the anger and crudeness had gone. Now he sounded like a little boy asking his mother's permission for something.

Mrs Talbot sat up. Her big breasts knocked against each other as she moved.

'Will you be all right?' she asked, her tone changed too.

He nodded. He looked drained. They exchanged looks. This whole performance had been a game, the chauffeur had been right, but it was a game in which Mrs Talbot, not her husband, had been the ringmaster. It was a game designed for her satisfaction, to meet her needs, her fantasy, not his. Perhaps tomorrow it would be his turn?

Without looking at Jason, Talbot wrapped the towel around his portly belly, kissed his wife on the cheek and trudged wearily out of the bedroom, closing the door behind him. Closing the door was a statement, closing Jason inside, telling him he didn't mind, didn't care what happened next.

'You want to go home?' Mrs Talbot said, using her fingers to restructure the bob in her shining blonde hair.

Jason hadn't the slightest idea what he wanted. His mind told him he had been used, a pawn in a game that went beyond their bedroom, that included the film, his screen test and Hanna Silverstein. Everything he had imagined, the worst case scenario, seemed to be true. Even Martha Morris's remark about thanking Hanna for loaning him to her, now seemed sinister. He had been brought to Los Angeles, not as an actor, but as a stud, as Hanna's new toy, to be passed around her friends and business partners.

That was what his mind told him. His body, on the other hand, always willing to betray him, told him that he was alone on a black sheeted bed with a beautiful blonde, his erection rock hard.

'You can stay,' she said matter-of-factly.

She reached out with her hand and ran the tips of her fingers down his chest until they reached his nipples.

'Good muscles. You do weights?' With the nails of her thumb and forefinger she pinched the nipple, pulling it away from his chest as though it were an elastic band. When it reached the limit of its elasticity she let go and it snapped back into place. She repeated the process with the other nipple. Jason felt a surge of raw passion.

'You can fuck me, or would you rather wank? I don't give head. Everyone in this town gives head but not me.'

As if to indicate her preference Mrs Talbot lay back on the bed. She jack-knifed her legs into the air and then opened them wide to form a long V. At the apex of the V was her sex. Looking at Jason all the time she slowly brought her ankles together again then drew her legs back until the top of her thighs pressed against the big pillows of her breasts. She hooked her hands round the back of her knees, pulling her legs back even more into a tight ball.

'Fuck me like this . . .'

In this position the whole of her sex was exposed, the fleshy labia, the puckered anus so recently used, the unusual width of the area between her legs. Her labia glistened. The mouth of her cunt was actually open, like the entrance to a dark cave, black and deep.

Jason felt his excitement racked up by this wantoness. He ran his finger up to the hood of her clitoris and delved underneath. He felt her respond with a shiver. His finger slid down to the entrance of her cunt. He watched himself push two fingers into the cave, then three, right in as far as they would go. He took them out again and moved down to her anus. He watched himself push two fingers in there too, then three. It felt hot and tight but just as wet as her cunt.

He felt oddly objective, as though all this hardly concerned him at all, as if this beautiful woman, rolled in a ball in front of him, so wantonly exposed, was a matter of indifference to him, like a scientific specimen laid out for experimentation. He saw himself touching her as though he were part of the experiment too.

He watched as his finger went back to her clitoris and began to circle it, drawing complex patterns of overlapping concentric rings on her delicate pink flesh.

He saw her eyes close. Her knuckles whitened as her fingers dug into the back of her knees, tightening their grip involuntarily, pulling her thighs back harder into her chest. He heard her voice, hard, serious, but almost as if it didn't belong to her at all.

'Don't stop that,' she said. 'Don't stop . . .'

He didn't. Still feeling remote and distant, an observer not a participant, he drew the circles around and over and alongside her clitoris with the very top of his finger. He was hardly touching her at all.

'Oh, oh . . .' he heard her moan. The crinkled labia pulsed visibly like the gills of a fish out of water. 'You bastard . . . you bastard . . . But then the orgasm overcame her and she could say or do nothing but hold on to herself, balled up as she was, hug herself tighter and feel the orgasm flood through her body. It was intense. In this position her cunt felt so open, while the rest of her was closed. It was as though her cunt was her mouth, breathing for her, sensing for her, living for her, while everything else was packed tightly away. That's how it felt. That's why she felt her labia quivering, why she thought she could feel her cunt itself opening up to the air, sucking it in.

Jason's mood changed so dramatically it was like a string breaking. One moment he was the detached observer, the next he had flung himself on to her body, rammed his cock into her open sex and was hammering into her as though demented.

His need was urgent. He wanted to think about nothing but spunking into her, into that so inviting sex, that he had studied in such detail. He didn't care what she felt. He didn't care about anything but his own need.

His chest was supported on the back of her thighs. His cock was deep inside her, in this position so deep he could feel the neck of her womb. There seemed to be a little ridge there, right inside those silky clinging walls, that rubbed against the rim of his glans. It was driving him wild with sensation. He had never felt it before. It was like a tiny finger there inside her, wanking him while he fucked. Her cunt was so tight, so hot, so wet. It was sucking him in. Sucking him on to that ridge where all his feelings were centred. He thought, somewhere, somehow, he felt her coming, her body contracting, her voice gasping, her sex opening even wider, but he didn't care. This was for him not her. He felt his cock beginning to spasm and made no attempt to hold back. Instead he drove harder until he felt his cock spit the first gob of spunk out. Then he stopped completely and waited for the spunk to explode into the liquid depths of her pulsating cunt and for his orgasm to take him down into the blackness where the only feeling would be unadulterated pleasure.

# Chapter Six

It was nine o'clock in the morning when the taxi dropped Jason off at Hanna's house in Beverly Hills. The journey from the Talbots' Gothic mansion had only taken twenty minutes. The black taxi driver had engaged him in conversation for most of the way.

'You English?'

'Yes.' Jason was not in a talkative mood.

'Actor?'

'How did you guess?'

'Man, you must be doing well. That house belongs to the most powerful man in Hollywood. So they say.'

'Really?'

'Sure thing. I'm an actor too. Wish I could get through his front door.'

'You're an actor?' That sparked Jason's interest.

'What, you don't recognise me?' He laughed.

'What have you done?'

'I've done two five-or-less in *New Columbo* and *Golden Girls*. And a ten-liner in *Law and Order*.'

'Five-or-less?'

'Five or less lines. Means you don't get residuals.'

'Where did you train?'

123

'Oh, I do classes down town. What you doing here, then?'

'Screen test for a Hanna Silverstein movie.'

'Hey, that's cool. How many are they testing?'

'What do you mean?'

'Say, you've got to know your opposition. Who else she testing? Is the part an English dude?'

'Don't know.'

'I heard she was in trouble. The studio wants names.'

'Names?'

'Stars. Above the title stars.'

'Oh. She's been talking to Martha Morris.'

'She don't mean nothin' any more. They'll have to do better than that.'

'You know a lot about it.'

'My man, this whole town's movies. I have people in the back talking about it all day and all night. This town's main industry isn't movies, it's gossip.'

'And what's the gossip about Hanna?' Jason wasn't sure he really wanted to know.

'Needs a hit.'

'I think she knows that.'

'Sure thing. She aren't stupid.'

The taxi was on the Talbots' account. But Jason realised he had no money for a tip. The black driver laughed when he told him.

'I'll add it to the bill,' he said.

'Sorry.'

'Give you a bit of advice for free, man.'

'What's that?'

'Watch your back.'

'What does that mean?'

'I heard there's an audition call at Burbank tomorrow.'

'And?'

'For *The Casting Couch* . . .'

'There's probably lots of parts.'

'Sure. Like I say, just watch your back. Have a nice day.'

The conversation did not improve Jason's mood. He was determined that after what had happened last night, he was going to have it out with Hanna. He was past the point of caring whether it meant being put on the next plane back to England. She was treating him like an object, a piece of property to be moved around for her convenience. He would be screen-tested no doubt – his night with the Talbots had presumably assured that – but he was beginning to doubt whether the screen test meant anything at all, especially after what the taxi driver had said. The screen test was a means to an end and the end was not giving him a part in her film.

In the house he ran upstairs to the bedroom. It was empty. He checked from a back window to see if Hanna was in the pool but the pool was empty too. He walked down to the terrace and tried the door of the private room they had made love in yesterday. It was locked. He banged on the door.

'Hanna, are you in there . . .'

He knocked again.

'Hanna . . .'

'Ms Hanna has gone to the studios, sir.' It was Maria. She stood in her black dress looking concerned.

'Do you know when she's coming back?'

'Tonight for sure. There's a party tonight.'

'What?'

'A party. The caterers will be coming soon. Big party for all her friends.'

'Here?'

'Si.'

'OK. Thanks, I'd better go to the studios to see her.'

'*Si, signor.*'

Maria walked back into the kitchen.

Jason went upstairs, showered and changed. As he pulled on a clean shirt he saw a large pantechnicon drive up to the house and around to the side entrance. Its logo, in big green letters on the side of the lorry, read: POURVOYEUR LE HAUTE CUISINE – DIDIER PAPAREMBORDE. He could hear voices and a clatter of activity as the lorry was unloaded.

Before he set off for the studios Jason decided to ring George Hammerstein. If he had managed to speak to Hanna on the phone the situation might just be clearer. If, even better, she had given him a definite idea of her intentions towards Jason, then the trip to the studios would be unnecessary. His ire and anger were beginning to evaporate slightly. With some reassurance that Hanna was going to treat him professionally he might well be able to forget what had happened. It would be stupid to take things too seriously. This was not London. Hollywood was a very different town.

On the phone he asked for George and got put through to Nancy.

'Hi, Jason.'

'Hi, Nancy. I was hoping to speak to George.'

'He's out right now.'

'Oh. Is there any news?'

'News?'

'Has he spoken to Hanna?'

'Oh. George is going to be away for a week.'

'That's sudden.'

'These things happen.' She sounded uncomfortable.

Jason felt disappointed. 'I need someone to clarify my situation, Nancy. It's important. Can you call her?'

'She wouldn't speak to me Jason.'

'Isn't there someone else who could?'

'Let me speak to Andy Cohen, George's partner.'

'Would you? I really want to get this sorted out.'

'Sure.'

'Soon?'

'I'll call you.'

'Thanks.'

'Don't mention it.'

Jason put the phone down and was instantly depressed. He got the impression that Hammerstein and Cohen were about as interested in him as they would be in a rotten fish. He didn't blame Nancy; she was obviously a junior in the organisation and, for whatever reason, George Hammerstein gave Jason's problems a very low priority.

Walking downstairs, seeing no alternative now but to talk to Hanna himself, he let himself out of the front door and started to walk down the driveway towards the garages. He hoped the map he had found in the glove compartment of the Mercedes would cover Burbank. He certainly couldn't remember the way from the limousine journey.

He had walked no more than ten feet when a bright yellow Lotus Elan skidded to a halt in the driveway in front of him, in a spray of gravel, and the unmistakable figure of Camilla Potts extracted herself from the low open-topped car.

'Jason!' she cried in delight, running over to him and kissing him on both cheeks as though he were a long lost friend.

'Camilla . . .' He had almost forgotten how beautiful she was. Despite all the lovely women he had seen in Hollywood Camilla was still in a class of her own. She had poise and grace and elegance. She moved like some sort of sleek, powerful, big cat. Her face was striking, high cheekbones, a perfectly proportioned nose and a sensual soft mouth. Her black hair cut to shoulder length was thick and shone with health. The attractions of her long lean body were not difficult to see. She wore a seamless sea-blue Lycra catsuit, her whole body covered in its figure hugging sheen. He could see those breasts he remembered so well, moulded by the tight material and flattened slightly against her chest. Down between her long legs the material even followed the crease of her sex. Her high heeled boots, in a matching blue, titled her pert arse into a firm pout.

'What are you doing here?' he asked, his concentration on what he was going to say to Hanna immediately dissipated.

'Hanna sent me.'

'Hanna. How long have you been back?'

'I got in yesterday. I'd have come to the party last night but I needed my beauty sleep. Come on. Let's open a bottle of champagne. It's really good to see you, Jason. I've been thinking about you.'

'It's good to see you too.' And judging by the way his pulse was racing, Jason meant it.

But it was not just a sexual impulse that made him glad to see her. For some reason Jason trusted Camilla. She was someone who he could really talk to, who would tell him the truth about where he stood in Hanna's life – professional and private.

They went into the house. Camilla was greeted enthusiastically by Maria.

'Bring us a bottle of champagne, will you, Maria,' Camilla asked. 'The good stuff. We're going out on the terrace.'

There were caterers everywhere, men and women, ferrying in chairs and tables, and boxes of glasses.

Out on the terrace they found a quiet spot away from all the mayhem. They sat at a little table in the sun.

'I've been thinking a lot about you,' Camilla said earnestly.

'Mutual,' he said, though it wasn't entirely true.

'Are you having a good time?'

'How do you mean, Hanna sent you?' he asked, ignoring her question.

'She rang me. Said she was busy all day and would I drop by and entertain you.'

Maria brought the champagne, 'the good stuff' being Dom Perignon, and two crystal champagne flutes on a silver tray. The bottle was in a silver wine cooler swathed in ice with a white linen napkin wrapped around its neck.

'I don't know what she could have meant, do you?' she said, standing up to open the bottle. She twisted the cork out expertly and poured the foaming wine without spilling a drop. She handed Jason a glass and sat down again. They clinked the glasses together and sipped the champagne.

'Very good,' he said.

'I love it.'

He could wait no longer to get it off his chest. 'I'm worried,

Camilla, he said, putting his glass down and looking straight into those dark brown eyes.

'I thought there was something wrong. Tell Aunty Camilla all about it.'

'I'm supposed to come here for a screen test, right?'

'Yep.'

'Hanna won't let me see a script. Won't tell me about the part. I've tried to get my agents to talk to her but they're playing some sort of game too. Or they're just not interested. I just don't think she is playing fair with me. She's using me.'

'Using you for what?'

It all came flooding out. He told her the full story, well almost the full story: Martha, the Talbots. He left out the details.

'Well, you have been seeing the sights, haven't you?' Camilla grinned broadly.

'Look, I like sex as much as anyone, it's just that . . .'

'I know. You feel used.'

'And I've heard rumours that I'm not the first . . .'

'Nor the last,' Camilla said casually.

'So what should I do?'

'That's easy isn't it?'

'Is it?'

'You have two choices, Jason. Simple. You either get on the next plane back to England. This afternoon.' She looked at her watch. 'Or you go with the flow.'

'And what does that mean?'

'Jason, Jason. So you have to fuck her and fuck her friends. So? If you get the screen test, if you get the part, it's all worthwhile. If you don't it's hardly the end of the world, is it? What have you lost? A bit of dignity is all. Your pride's hurt.

Come on, this is the nineties. Men can be used sexually just like women. That's female liberation for you.'

'Which means what?'

'Stick it out. Play her game. The better you are the more likely she is to use you in the film. Fuck your way to the top . . .' She laughed, then picked up her glass of champagne. 'Here's to success.'

He was not entirely convinced but he toasted success anyway. Perhaps she was right, though his professional pride was not so easily assuaged. Idealistically, he'd wanted to star in a film not because he'd fucked the producer but because he was a talented actor who had been right for the part. It looked as though his standards and the Hollywood norm were two very different things.

Camilla stood up, her long legs looking wonderfully shapely in the clinging blue sheen of the Lycra. He could see the curve of her pubic bone as it dipped between her thighs.

'And talking of fucking,' she said, taking his hand and pulling him to his feet. 'There's something I want to show you.'

She handed him the two champagne flutes, picked the champagne bottle out of the cooler and led him past the swimming pool and down the landscaped gardens. A gardener, sitting on a tractor mower, was cutting the sloping lawns. The sun seemed hotter today, the haze of smog that usually hung in the air less thick.

They were heading for the summerhouse. Jason would have liked to suggest that they went upstairs to the bedroom. It would serve Hanna right if he fucked this gorgeous creature on Hanna's bed. But Camilla appeared to have other ideas.

The main door of the summerhouse had a computer lock. Camilla punched three numbers into the control panel and the door sprung open. Just before he followed Camilla inside Jason noticed a small black van parked outside the garage complex. What it was doing there he had no idea, until he remembered the caterers. It must belong to them.

Camilla beckoned him in, closing the door firmly behind her. He tried to read the expression on her face. It was excitement, that much was clear, but it was coloured with something else, something he couldn't read, or even guess at.

She pushed him back against the door with her body. Her height and the high-heeled boots put her mouth almost level with his. Pressing her body into his she kissed him full on the mouth, her tongue thrusting between his lips. Her body felt soft and pliable.

'Oh, Jason . . . God I want you,' she said, breaking away from his mouth.

'Let's go back to the house then . . .'

'No, Jason. There's no need. There's something I have to say to you first.'

'What?'

'It's difficult.' She would not meet his eyes.

He looked down into the summerhouse. They were in a narrow corridor. It reminded him of the sort of hall that led to squash courts or gymnasiums, functional white walls, vinyl tiled floors, doors with round portholes of frosted glass. There were three doors in all. It didn't look very condusive to sex.

'Can't we go somewhere more comfortable?' he asked.

Camilla took the glasses from his hand and poured out more champagne.

'Jason . . . do you want to please me, pleasure me?'

'Of course, that's why I think we should go . . .'

'It's just that . . .'

'What?'

'I'm not like other women. I have very different needs. Special needs. You might not understand.'

After the last two days he thought he understood only too well.

'Whatever you want . . .'

'I know what I want, what turns me on . . .'

'I want to please you . . .' That was true. All this talk was making his imagination run riot. His erection was already tenting his slacks. 'You only have to tell me.'

'Finish your champagne,' she said, coolly drinking hers down to the bottom of the glass. He did the same. She set the bottle down on the corridor floor and put the glasses down next to it. Then she took his hand and led him down the corridor to the door at the far end. She opened it but only a fraction. Hung against the door on the inside was a thick velvet curtain. It prevented the door being opened by more than a foot or so. They squeezed through the gap.

The lights were already on in the room, a series of halogen spotlights creating stark pools of white light in some areas, while others remained in almost total darkness. The whole room was draped in thick velvet, a dark shade of burgundy. On one wall there was a large mirror but apart from that the folds of the curtaining covered every inch of wall. A deep pile carpet was laid on the floor in a matching colour and the ceiling too had been painted in the same dark red. The carpet and drapes deadened the sound.

But it was not this peculiar decoration that took Jason's attention. It was what the room contained. Standing in one of the pools of light was a wooden slatted frame the size of a small double bed. At each of its corners were metal hoops to which leather straps were attached. A thick leather strap was secured to the middle slat and lay unbuckled on the frame. In another pool of light was a plain upright carved chair, its back extending well above where any occupant's head would rest. The seat of the chair had been cut away so it resembled a horseshoe. Leather straps had been screwed into the arms, around the front legs, and at the back of the chair at what would be waist, chest and neck level.

There were two more items lit by the spotlights. The first was a wooden trestle, the bar across its top padded in suede. Leather straps were attached to each of its four splayed legs at their feet. The second item was a vast wardrobe, an ancient French walnut armoire which was sited against one wall. Its doors were open. Hanging from the back of the doors Jason could see a selection of whips and leather paddles as well as leather harnesses, straps and handcuffs. Inside there appeared to be a variety of leather and rubber clothing, as well as lace, satin and silk lingerie of all types.

'What is this?'

'Are you shocked?'

'No.'

'It was Hanna's idea. When either of us were in the mood to play games. Only her and I have the combination.'

'Hanna's into this?'

'Sometimes. Not as much as me.'

'Jason,' she said seriously. 'I'm one of those people who

take my pleasure from pain. I'm a masochist.'

'What does that mean?'

'It's OK. You don't have to stay. Why don't you just say you're horrified and leave?'

'I'm not horrified,' he said slowly. He was much too aroused to want to leave.'

'Will you help me then . . .'

'Help you?'

'Be my master. Play a part for me, Jason. Be my master. You're an actor. Act it for me.'

'I don't know how.'

'Surely you know what to do with a slave. That's what I want to be. Your slave.'

She kissed him hard on the mouth again, deliberately biting his lip until it hurt. Before he could react she danced away. She went to the wooden trestle and laid herself over it, putting her wrists and ankles into the leather straps as if to demonstrate.

The blue Lycra stretched tightly over her buttocks, the material clearly pressed into the crease of her sex. She straightened up and went to lie on the wooden frame. She spread-eagled herself on it, once again pushing her wrists and ankles into the open leather restraints, her body taut. She gasped slightly as if her imagination had run away with her.

She sat in the chair next, her back straight, her head up as if it were held by the strap at her neck. Jason could see her excitement. Her eyes sparkled.

'You have to take control. That's my turn on, Jason. That's what I love. Letting someone else take control. You have to make me do what you want. Master.'

Half of him wanted only to go, to take her back to the house,

take her up to the bedroom and fuck her there. No games. No
fantasies. No slaves or masters. Half of him was caught in the
trap, fascinated to see where this bizarre game would end.

'You'd better take your clothes off then. Or do you want me
to tear them off?' He tried to sound masterful. That was the
role she wanted him to play and he was supposed to be an
actor, wasn't he? He doubted that they'd ever given classes at
RADA in this sort of performance.

In one of the dark corners of the room there was a three-
panelled screen also upholstered in burgundy. Camilla
disappeared behind it.

Jason went to the cupboard. He opened one of its drawers
which contained a variety of stockings and suspender belts.
Another he opened was full of dildoes of every conceivable
type and size – except silver, of course. He examined the whips.
He knew this world existed. He had read about it. But he'd
never been involved before. His mind was full of questions.
How long had Camilla been into all this? And Hanna? What
was her penchant?

But for the moment, as during the last few days, it was
his body, not his mind, that was propelling him forward. He
wanted Camilla badly. He wanted to see her naked again,
renew his memory of that magnificent body he'd seen in
the mirrors of the hotel bathroom. He wanted to take her,
fuck her.

'No!' her voice rang out from behind the screen, its sharp
edge muffled by the velvet. 'No . . . please.'

She was ready. Now he had to play his role. He needed a
prop. He plucked a short leather riding crop off the walnut
door of the cupboard.

136

'Come out where I can see you,' he ordered, trying to sound masterful again.

'No.'

'Do it.'

'No.'

He strode behind the screen. Camilla was naked. He caught her wrist and pulled her out into the pool of light.

'Please don't hurt me,' she said.

'Stand still.'

She obeyed. She looked genuinely frightened. Her body was even better than he'd remembered it. Her uptilted breasts were rich orbs of flesh, her waist pinched, her navel iron-flat, and the runnel of her sex completely unobstructed by hair. Suddenly Jason felt a thrill of pleasure run through his body. This beautiful woman wanted him to control her, use her. She had granted him power over her.

He stood back and released her hand.

'Turn round,' he ordered.

She turned slowly. He watched as that pert apple-shaped arse came into view, its plumpness emphasised by the depth of its cleft.

'If you don't do everything I tell you, it'll be the worst for you.' That line sounded like something from a fifties pirate movie. He tried to give it conviction.

'Yes, master,' she said quietly.

'I am your master.' He picked up the cue. 'Now bend over the trestle.'

'Please don't gag me, master,' she begged.

'Get me a gag.' He picked up the clue. It was like Brer Rabbit asking not to be thrown into the briar patch.

Camilla took a gag from the cupboard. It was a leather strap with a ball of rubber screwed into its centre. Jason took it from her and strapped it in place, buckling it tight around her brunette hair. Now he was on his own.

'Over . . .' he said.

She obeyed immediately, her tall frame bending almost double over the splayed legs, her ankles and wrists against its leather straps.

In this position the whole of her hairless sex was open and exposed. He had never seen a woman with no hair on her labia. He could see every detail under the white light of the spotlight, the puffy wrinkled outer lips, the tight pink inner ring, the hood of her clitoris like the head of a tiny snake, and the puckered corona of her anus, like the crater of an extinct volcano.

He knelt by the frame and strapped her wrists securely to the foot of the trestle. The gag held her hair out of her eyes, otherwise it would have obscured her view. He could see her excitement as he cinched her wrists into the straps but once again he thought there was something else in her eyes he could not read.

It was a matter of seconds before her wrists and ankles were secured in the padded leather straps.

He got to his feet. This is what she wanted, he kept telling himself. He could hear her voice in his head: 'I take pleasure in pain.' It was all new to him.

In no particular hurry he stripped off his clothes. His erection bobbed out in front of him. He wanked it inquisitively a couple of times to see how it felt. It felt hard. However new the situation his cock seemed to be in no doubt about what it should do.

He stroked the curve of Camilla's arse. There was a

sharpness about it where her thighs bent away from her pelvis, not enough padding to cover its tautness. He knew she wanted to be whipped. He'd never struck a woman before. Tentatively he raised his hand and slapped it down on her arse. The movement made his cock tremble. Camilla moaned, a moan he could hear was pure pleasure. He could see the lips of her cunt throbbing. Almost before he realised what he was doing he raised the riding crop and stroked it down across her buttocks. She moaned louder, the gag making the sound seem all the more uncontrolled. In rapid succession he stroked the writhing arse six times, producing six well-defined red welts across her lightly tanned hide.

She was moaning continuously, the exposed lips of her cunt twitching out of control. There was no doubt in his mind that she had come. It had made her come.

He stood between her legs and nudged his cock into her labia. With the only movement she could make, she pushed herself back on to him. He could feel the heat the welts were generating.

Her cunt seemed to have a life of its own. It was groping for him like some hungry mouth groping for food. He pressed his cock into it and it sucked him in voraciously. He heard another muffled moan. The depths of her sex were liquid, molten, like heaving molten lava.

Using all her strength she struggled against her bonds, wanting to feel her constriction. She screamed obscenities at him through the gag though not more than an incomprehensible babble could be heard. The bondage turned her on, fighting against the gag turned her on. She was coming again, or just extending the orgasm she'd experienced with the beating, she didn't know or care. His cock, hard and stout, was right up inside her, her arse cheeks burning from the whip, pushing against his navel. She had no control. This was her fantasy. Bound and helpless. Her body plunged into orgasm as she squeezed herself around the sword of his cock.

Jason pulled away. He looked down on his cock, glistening with her juices. The game was over. It was no longer a performance. He knew the role now; like any good actor, it had become part of him. He no longer had to think about what to do.

Leaving Camilla prone over the trestle he went to the wardrobe and searched for a prop. He found what he was looking for, a face mask, shaped to the forehead, large holes for the eyes and nose, exaggerated cheeks but cut short above the mouth, so mouth and chin were exposed. It was some sort of plastic covered with black leather. He strapped it tightly over his face. The perfect prop. He looked like the Master, the black-faced Master. He saw his face in the mirror and smiled a sinister smile. His steely blue eyes looked back at him through the eye slots.

He knelt and released Camilla from her bonds. He told her to take her gag out. Her big breasts quivered as she straightened up and raised her arms to unbuckle the strap at the back of her head.

'What now, Master?' she said, watching his eyes in the mask. The mask changed his face, made him look cruel. She felt a shiver run through her body as she looked at him.

'Whatever I choose . . .' His voice was different, high and reedy. He sat on the edge of the slatted wooden frame. 'Kneel. Lick my cock but don't take it in your mouth.'

She knelt in front of his open legs. With long thick strokes of her tongue she lapped at his cock, tasting the saltiness of her own juices. She licked his balls. They were soaked with her taste too, his pubic hair wet from it.

'Your pleasure now, Master,' she said.

'Yes. My pleasure . . .'

It was his turn. He pushed her with his hand on her shoulder so she sprawled backward on the thick carpet. She had fallen out of the circle of light that illuminated the wooden frame. Immediately she scrambled round the frame until she was lit again.

'I didn't tell you to move.' He hadn't ordered her to do that.

'Please, Master, you have to see me. See my shaven pussy. Do you like my pussy?' She stroked it with both her hands, her legs spread wide apart.'

'I didn't tell you to do that either,' he said querulously.

'Punish me then, Master.' She turned on her stomach and thrust her arse into the air, the long slit of her sex a deep channel between the cliffs of her buttocks.

Jason slashed the whip across her arse. She deserved it this time, she had disobeyed the Master. He stroked the whip three times. Each time it hit her solidly in the middle of her buttock, each time, with no gag now, she cried out with a noise that seemed to him to express a sort of animal ecstasy.

The whipping made her come again, lying on the carpet, writhing herself against it, out of control, moaning and squirming herself against the floor, her breasts hard against the carpet, her hand down between her legs, brutally wanking her clitoris until the orgasm erupted and flooded her nerves.

Jason dropped to his knees, threw the whip aside, seized

her by the hips and pulled her back on to him. His cock sunk into her cunt but he knew that was not what he wanted. He pulled it out and moved it up to the tiny mouth of her anus.

'Oh yes, yes . . .' she screamed.

He didn't need her approval. He thrust forward, not caring if he hurt her. He was too close to his climax now, his balls churning, his mind full of all he'd felt and seen and done. He saw the whip landing on her unprotected buttocks, saw how she had squirmed and come on it, heard the thwack of leather on flesh. All new to him, all pushing him to the brink. Without caring for anything but his own completion he pushed deep into her, pulling her hips back on to him to go as deep as he could.

With no gag the noise she was making was almost deafening. She was screaming, gasping, moaning 'bugger me, bugger me', her head up, looking straight into the mirror in front of them so she could see his face in the mask and his muscles rippling as he used them to thrust into her. Then her eyes rolled back, and another orgasm broke over his cock.

He came too, came deep in the hot tight arse, every muscle in his body locked, his hands like iron claws on her hips, his eyes watching her magnificent body in the mirror, her tits sweeping the carpet as they bounced up and down, watching until his eyes were forced to close by the dark, rich, unlimited pleasure that came as his spunk spurted out into her intimate depths.

'He's come.'
'Has he.'
'Look.'

'I thought he was supposed to pull out and come over her ass, not inside her. The punters like to see it. Otherwise they think it's faked.'

'That's what he was supposed to do.'

'Still, it's not bad stuff.'

'We should have seen the spunk . . .'

'Well, it's still pretty good. That Camilla's really something. She actually gets off on it.'

'She fakes it just like all the rest.'

'No way. Come on, that's not faking it. She's into pain. That whipping . . .'

'Who knows?'

'I know. Christ I've seen enough fakes doing this for three years. She ain't faking it, take it from me.'

'Yah, you may be right.'

'If she's faking it, man, she's the best goddamn actress in the whole of Hollywood.'

'Yah. OK, OK.'

'Is that it then?'

'Don't know. You think she can get him to do it again?'

'I'd love to have a go at her.'

'Don't tell me you're getting horny?'

'I'm horny for her. That shaven pussy really turns me on.'

'She's a looker, all right.'

The two men stared through the two-way mirror. Jason had taken off the mask and was lying next to Camilla on the carpet. Her head was resting against his chest.

'No, I think that's a wrap.'

'Why?'

'Instinct.'

'Ten dollars she'll get it up again.'

'You're on.'

'Better clean the glass again. It's hot in here. It's getting a bit steamed.'

One man wiped the glass clean while his companion changed the cassette in the camera. It was just as well he did. An hour later as they climbed into their black van, with two video cassettes filled with action safely in the cameraman's case, his assistant took a ten dollar bill from his wallet.

'It was worth it,' he said.

'That Camilla. She's a star.'

'What guy could resist?'

# Chapter Seven

Hanna arrived home at six, by which time her house had been transformed by Didier Paparemborde's company. The main reception room, opening on to the terrace and garden, had been turned into a bar and buffet, tables draped in pink tablecloths and matching flounces and pleats and elaborate bows. Out on the terrace fifty or sixty tables had been arranged, each individually set with white china and sparkling glass and pink napkins pressed into the shape of swans. Over every available branch and shrub a long flex had been draped which contained tiny bulbs that would shine like stars in the firmament, creating a romantic atmosphere. Large industrial heaters were artfully concealed in the bushes to raise the ambient temperature of the garden to seventy-five degrees Fahrenheit, in the event that Nature should let a late evening chill develop.

There were flowers everywhere. Lilies had been floated in the swimming pool together with little bowls holding night lights, their flames providing further twinkling background moodiness. Each table was provided with a bouquet of flowers at its centre, co-ordinated to the subtle pink of the tablecloth. There were two man-sized arrangements of flowers on either side of the terrace doors.

A twenty-piece band, all wearing the same pink and white

suits, were setting up on the lawn at the side of the pool ready to recreate the music of Glenn Miller and Tommy Dorsey until eleven o'clock, at which time the elder members of the band would go home and the younger transform themselves into an eight-piece rock band heavily influenced by Billy Joel. The people who appreciated forties music were calculated to be the people who left parties early. Rock was for the youngsters who would stay late.

Didier had supervised the food personally. The ingredients had been flown in on a Boeing 747 last night from his home town of Menton in the South of France. This gave his food - at least according to his publicity - the genuine taste of France. In addition, the cuisine of Provence, so popular in Hollywood at the moment, was given a special twist with a distinct Italian influence, Menton being so near the border. At least that's what the publicity said. Cold pasta in lobster sauce, red pepper salad, ratatouille, focaccia bread, and fish salad were among the specialties. Along one side of the terrace two barbecues had been set up to grill sea bass on dried cuttings from the vines of the Bandol. Of course there were also hamburgers and Caesar salad for the less discerning palates.

Jason had found a sanctuary from the bustle of activity in a small downstairs room next to the kitchen - since the caterer's had brought their own mobile kitchens the kitchen was the quietest place in the house - and was trying to understand the intricacies of baseball, without that much success.

'Jason . . .' Hanna said. 'That's where you're hiding.'

'Hi.' he said. He hadn't seen her since the party last night and hadn't decided what his attitude to her was going to be. His activities with Camilla had rather overshadowed his anger.

'You had a good day?' she smiled what he took to be a knowing smile. The relationship between Camilla Potts and Hanna Silverstein was still a mystery to him; but he wouldn't be surprised if Camilla had talked to Hanna on the phone after she left him.

'Camilla came round.'

'I know. Come upstairs with me . . .'

She held out her hand. Her mood seemed gentle, like first thing in the morning. He got up and took her hand. She squeezed it affectionately and they went upstairs hand in hand.

In the bedroom she kicked off her shoes, slumped on the bed, made a pile of pillows to lean on and put her feet up, patting the sheet besides her for Jason to join her.

'Been a hard day,' she said.

'Really?'

'Sometimes I think I should give it all up. Go and live on a South Sea island.'

'It gets to you, does it?'

'Sure does.'

She picked up his hand again and squeezed it, closing her eyes for a moment. Her over-tanned face was lined, the pressures of the day etched, like engraving on glass.

Jason, against the odds, felt a surge of affection for this woman. He had never known anyone change moods so dramatically but when she was like this, when she allowed herself to be vulnerable, it was impossible not to feel sympathy for her.

He stroked her hand softly.

'Nice . . .' she murmured. 'I should take a shower . . .' But she didn't move.

He ran his fingers up to her naked arm. She was wearing a sleeveless shirt-waister dress, once again in white. It was belted at the waist by a gold chain. His hand unbuttoned the top of the dress and slipped inside on to her white silk bra.

'Nicer . . .' she mouthed. He found her nipple and teased it until it was erect. He repeated the process with the other breast. She turned her head to one side, away from him, pressing her cheeks into the downy pillow.

Jason unfastened the remaining buttons of the dress and unhooked the gold chain. She wore only a pair of white French knickers, no tights, no slip. He slid his hand over her navel, feeling the silkiness of the knickers on his palm. His fingers curled around her pubic bone, moulding itself to the shape of the sharp angle at the apex of her thighs, his fingers pushing down between her legs.

'Nicer still . . .' she said smiling.

'Shall I continue?' he asked.

This was not what he'd imagined he'd be doing at all. He had prepared several speeches. They all began, 'Now look Hanna . . .' and ended, ' . . . or else I'm going to get on the next plane back to England.' None of them envisaged this scenario. Especially not after this session with Camilla. But feeling her body was giving him an erection . . .

'Oh baby . . .' she said, by way of reply, as she eased her legs apart so his hand was free to stroke the silk between her thighs. He used the silk, pressed it into her labia, so she would feel its slippery, sensual texture.

'So nice . . .'

'Just relax.'

'That's not going to relax me, Jason. That's going to get me all worked up.'

'I'll stop then,' he teased.

'No. No. I love it. Do it to me, baby . . .'

He eased the crotch of the knickers to one side and gently, with only the very tip of his finger, found her clitoris. He touched it as lightly as he could, the brush of a butterfly's wing.

Hanna moaned.

He made little circles around the tiny mountain of feeling. He nudged it, pressed it, probed it, explored the valleys that surrounded it, climbed to its summit. It was hot.

His erection hardened, trapped uncomfortably in the folds of his trousers.

'I'm going to take my clothes off,' he said.

'Yes . . .'

For the second time that day he stripped off his shirt and slacks, his shoes and socks and pants. Hanna opened her eyes and turned to watch him. His cock, its circumcised head weeping a tear of fluid in excitement, was smooth and large, his balls big too, the blond pubic hair as light as the hair on his head.

'Very pretty. All those muscles . . .' She felt a thrill of anticipation.

He sat back on the bed and reached for the waistband of her knickers. She raised her hips off the bed and he pulled them clear. His hand went to unfasten her bra.

'No,' she said quietly. 'Leave it.' She offered no explanation and he asked for none.

His hand returned to the sparse triangle of hair and the hard bone of her pubis. She was wet now. He toyed gently with her labia, then penetrated her with just one finger. Crooking his finger he caressed the wet velvety wall of her cunt.

'Oh yes, yes . . .' she said loudly, enthusiastically. 'Do that.'

He worked his finger against the spot he had found, feeling his fingernail scratching at what felt exactly like wet velvet. There appeared to be nothing to differentiate this from any other part of her sex but it was clearly driving Hanna wild. From lying passively, her whole body had tensed and she was writhing on the bed, tossing her head from side to side, whimpering, and, when she could manage to form the words, begging him not to stop.

He didn't. He worked his finger methodically, rhythmically and watched as her body climaxed, its nerves taking her over, satisfying their own demands, making her do what they wanted to do. Instinctively Jason put his other hand on to her pubis, his finger against her clitoris, touching it gently. That, for her already tortured senses, was the last straw. Assailed by feelings from her G-spot and her clitoris, both together, she arched up off the bed, as her world blanked out and all she could experience was exquisite sensation.

As he felt the tension drain from her Jason eased his finger from her body.

'So good . . .' Hanna said. 'No one's ever found it before. I didn't think I had one.'

'One what?'

'A G-spot. Wasn't that what you were doing?'

'You want the truth or shall I lie?'

'I don't care either way. It was great. Now it's your turn.' Her hand snaked out and grabbed at his penis. She pulled it towards her, leaving him in no doubt what she wanted. He rolled on top of her.

'Give it to me, Jason, let yourself go, baby . . .'

Her hand guided his cock down between her legs until he felt it at the mouth of her cunt. He plunged it forward. Immediately her hand let go of his shaft and probed down to find his balls. He started a rhythm. Her fingers closed around his scrotum, reeling in one ball and then the other, until she had them cupped firmly in the palm of her hand. She squeezed them gently, then pulled them down and away from his body. It was a wonderful sensation. He felt it in his cock, his skin stretched back. It was as though he had a foreskin and she was peeling it away. It made his cock somehow more sensitive. It churned his spunk.

She wanted to make him come. His nipples were areas no one had explored on his body, she knew that from before. Raising her head from the pillow she positioned herself so she could sink her mouth over his hard nipple. She played with it, flicking it with her tongue. He reacted instantly, his body shuddering. She closed her teeth around it and bit sharply. He reacted again, another involuntary shudder.

'Come, baby . . .' she whispered, then bit again, as her hand pulled at his balls, trying to milk the spunk out of him.

He could take no more. He felt his spunk rising, as her teeth tortured his nipple. It was like she knew how to tenderise him, make him feel more, make his cock and his nipples so sensitive he could not resist the urge to spunk however hard he tried, however much his exertions with Camilla had taken out of him. His cock jerked inside her, jerking against her hand too where it held his balls so tightly. She squeezed his balls one final time, bit his nipple just as his spunk flooded into her cunt, his orgasm infinite, feelings he had never felt before.

They lay side by side on the bed without saying anything. Hanna had rested her head on his shoulder and he'd wrapped his arm around her back. Her hand lay on his chest. Their breathing was deep and synchronised, just on the edge of sleep.

But the clatter of activity from downstairs was too insistent to allow them to go under completely.

'Better get ready,' Hanna said, sitting up, the white silk bra still enclosing her small breasts. She kissed Jason on the cheek. 'Actually I'd like to cancel the whole damn thing and spend the night in bed with you.'

Jason saw his opportunity. He quickly rephrased the speech he had rehearsed.

'Hanna, I really need to talk to you.'

'Baby, baby, I know what you're going to say. And it's all my fault. Camilla called me. She wanted to help. She's very fond of you.'

'I thought . . .'

'It's just I've been under so much pressure with this film. Talbot's a bastard, Jason. A complete bastard. When he saw you . . . Well, what could I do? In this town when that man says jump everyone asks how high. That's this goddamn awful business. If I lose him, I lose the film. So you made him happy. I get my picture. You get the test, and you'll be great . . .'

'You said that before'

'Definite, baby. I'm going to organise it first thing tomorrow. I got some rewrites today. There's a good scene we can use.'

'What about George Mason?'

'What about him?'

'Is he going to direct the test?'

'If that's what you want? It'll have to be in the morning. After twelve he's too drunk.'

'I think he should . . .'

'Sure. But I decide who's going to be in my pictures, not Mason. Mason points the cameras, that's about all he's good for.'

'Can I see the script then, if you got rewrites?'

'Sure. Tomorrow. That's a promise, baby.' She patted his cheek. 'And . . .'

'Yes?'

'I'm really sorry. I mean it. Treating you this way. Especially when you've been so good to me. You must think I'm a complete bitch.'

'Well I . . .'

She kissed him on the mouth preventing him finishing his sentence.

'New beginnings. Let's get changed and then we can drink to new beginnings.'

The band played 'Moonlight Serenade' followed by 'In The Mood'. Jason wore his dark suit and black shirt again. Hanna had squeezed into a clinging full length white dress that was decorated with thousands of little spangles sown in a swirling pattern around the semi-elastic material. Once again she drank nothing but bourbon. Once again she did not appear to expect Jason to be at her side and wandered around from guest to guest leaving him to his own devices. Not that he minded. After their talk in the bedroom he was feeling distinctly optimistic. Not only had she answered all his questions, she had apologised and appeared genuinely contrite. When it came down to it, as far as the Talbots were concerned he could hardly protest with too much righteous indignation. It wasn't as though Mrs Talbot had been exactly unattractive or that he'd been asked to do something a thousand men, a hundred thousand, wouldn't have given their right arm to do.

Since he'd arrived in Hollywood he had realised that the attitude to sex was completely different from the English one. There were different mores, a different approach to life and, more crucially for him, to work. Well, he decided, when in Rome . . .

Waitresses carried trays of champagne glasses and canapés among the throng of guests. They were dressed as Apache dancers, black satin skirts slit almost to the waist, fish-net stockings underneath, blouses heaving with the large bosoms that appeared to be compulsory in Hollywood.

'How about a dance.' A hand had tapped Jason on the shoulder. He turned to see Martha Morris grinning at him enthusiastically. Her red hair and been curled into tight waves, her red dress was no more than a tube of stretchy material, a shiny silk, pulled over her ample bosom and down to the middle of her thighs, with only two thin spaghetti straps to support it. At her neck she wore a simple silver choker with a large diamond set in its centre.

'Hi.'

'You look very dapper.'

'You look wonderful.'

'Dance with me, then.'

He took her hand and walked out on to the terrace where a space had been cleared for dancing. Several couples smooched around the floor to the big band sound, their degree of intimacy expressed by the way they held each other. Two or three of the men had their fingers buried in the flesh of their partners' rumps. One couple danced while they kissed, mouth to mouth, their eyes closed, circling the same foot of ground.

Martha rested her hands in the small of his back. He could hardly bear to look into her cleavage, remembering graphically what he had used it for. She made sure their bodies pushed together, her thigh straying between his legs. After five minutes of this he decided enough was enough.

'Let me get you a drink,' he said, breaking out of her arms.

'What's the matter? Afraid Hanna might be watching? She gave me carte blanche, remember?'

'Don't I get a vote?'

'Jason. Don't tell me you're objecting. I'd be offended. Are you trying to tell me you didn't enjoy . . .'

'Of course not.'

'Well then.'

'You're a very beautiful woman. And very successful. You could have anybody.'

'Exactly. So you should feel flattered.'

'Why me?'

'Firstly because you're a great fuck and secondly because you're new blood.'

'New blood?'

'This is Hollywood, Jason. Don't look so shocked. You may be on the way up. That would be good for me.'

Jason took two glasses of champagne from a passing waitress and they walked back into the house, Martha's arm slipped into his.

'And talking of what's good for us. over there. Now there's a couple you have to meet if you're going to get on in this town.'

In the corner of the room, sitting on a small sofa were two people who, at first, Jason took to be a married couple. It was only as Martha led him over to them that he realised that what he had taken to be a man was in fact a woman immaculately dressed as a man, in a double-breasted pin stripped suit, white shirt and tie with a sparkling diamond tie-pin holding the silk tie in place. As Martha approached the suited woman got to her feet.

'Martha darling,' she said, her voice as masculine as her appearance. Her hair was slicked back with haircream, parted like a man's and looked as if it had been dyed a darker black.

'Harry,' Martha replied. They kissed on each cheek, making extravagant kissing noises though their lips made no contact with skin. Martha held Jason's hand tightly so he could not escape. He had an overwhelming desire to do just that.

'Harry Teitelbaum, this is Jason . . . forgotten, darling . . .'
'MacIver.'
'MacIver, that's it. Jason, Harriet Teitelbaum.'

Harriet held out her hand and shook Jason's with the briefest possible movement.

'Oh, he's very pretty,' she said to Martha.

The woman who had been sitting next to Harry on the sofa rose to her feet. She was a blonde, with hair that looked as though it had been bleached so many times it had no natural life left in it. She was much younger than Harry, perhaps as young as nineteen, and was one of the few women Jason had met in Hollywood who did not have a massive bosom. Her tits were nicely shaped but small. It was easy to see this since the dress she was wearing was completely transparent, a black net of material on to which various brightly coloured brooches had been sewn, though none in strategic places. Had she not been wearing a pair of sleek black panties, Jason would have been able to see whether she was a natural blonde. As it was he could see every detail of her body apart from the area under the panties.

'Hello,' she said in a light squeaky voice.

'Hi Cyn, how's things?' Martha asked.

'Like usual.' Cynthia looked at Jason. They were not introduced.

'This is Hanna's latest discovery,' Martha explained.

'Very pretty. No wonder she's looking so happy this evening.'

'I've had him on loan already.'

'Had being the operative word, knowing you, Martha.'

Jason could not believe what he was hearing. He tried to break out of Martha's grip but couldn't do it without drawing attention to himself. Once again it was as though he had ceased to exist, an inanimate object to be discussed at will.

'Definitely. The queue forms behind me.'

Martha lent forward and whispered something into Harriet Teitelbaum's ear. Harriet's eyes never left Jason's body for a moment. As Martha spoke he saw them drop to his crotch.

'Oh, I think I'd like that,' Harry said.

'Can we get another drink?' Cyn asked.

'Of course, my darling. Excuse us.' Harry took Cynthia's hand and they walked over to the bar.

'What did you say?' Jason asked angrily.

'Christ, what's the matter with you? Do you know who that was? Harriet Teitelbaum, for Christ's sake. She's number two in this town. Some say number one. She finances at least half the pictures that get made. If she likes you . . . well . . . My God, I'd sleep with her at the drop of a hat. I'm just not her type. She likes young chicks like Cyn.'

'What did you say?' Jason insisted, trying to keep calm.

'Jason, pour some water on it. This is Hollywood. You've got to lighten up. Be Hollywood. If I were in London I'd behave differently. But this is here.'

'So what did you tell her?'

'The truth. That you're a great lay.'

'But you said she's a lesbian.'

'I don't know what she is. She dresses like this lesbian butch dike. Always has. She's always got some waif in tow like Cyn. But I don't know what she does for kicks. Maybe you'll get lucky. Maybe we'll both get lucky. We could give them a show, couldn't we? And there's definitely a part in her next film for me. My agent's read the script . . .'

Jason started to laugh. He looked at Martha Morris and laughed louder. In his eyes she was one of the most important stars in Hollywood, an international name, known by millions of people. She was thought of as the epitome of beauty, elegance and sophistication and here she was talking like a whore in a brothel hoping the client would pick her from the line up.

To her credit she stared laughing too. 'I told you, that's Hollywood. You better learn fast if you want to get on.'

'Well now I know it's true.'

'And at least you've got all the credentials for success. How 'bout a quickie in the bushes?'

'And risk being found by Hanna. That wouldn't do either of our careers any good, would it?'

'She gave me permission, remember?'

'And you believed her?'

Jason looked into her wonderful green eyes and saw them register doubt.

She laughed. 'You learn fast.'

They danced some more and then Martha was taken off by a bespectacled and earnest young man who told her he'd written a screenplay especially for her about a female prison officer trying to work in a male jail. She appeared fascinated by this unlikely proposition and took him off into a corner to talk about it.

Jason drank some more champagne. Among the guests he recognised several 'star' faces like Martha. Some looked a great deal better than they did on screen, others a great deal worse. Everywhere he looked there seemed to be beautiful women, the similarity between their figures testament to the exercise, health and fitness regimens everyone seemed to practise, as well as the financial success of numerous orthodontists and plastic surgeons. Big breasts, neat buttocks, slim waists and legs were the norm. Faces too, symmetrical noses, pert chins, raised cheekbones, pouting lips and wide eyes, were also ubiquitous. There was also a high proportion of blondes.

From across the terrace Jason saw Hanna sitting at one of the tables talking to three elderly men, all of whom were Japanese. A fourth man was slumped forward on the table, his head resting on his arms, sleeping deeply. It was George Mason.

Jason had seen no sign of Camilla Potts. He realised that

she had not mentioned seeing him later, as she'd left. Presumably she had another engagement.

In need of a pee and finding the downstairs cloakroom occupied, and with two people waiting, Jason decided to use the loo in the master bedroom suite. He walked up the curving staircase. Gradually as he found his way into the bathroom the noise of the party below diminished. He set his glass down on the vanity unit, unzipped his trousers and extracted his cock. He peed in a hard stream.

'I thought I might find you in here.'

The voice surprised him so much he only just managed to stop himself spraying piss over the white marble floor.

'Don't mind me.'

Mrs Talbot walked right up to the toilet bowl and stood beside him looking down at his cock. She was wearing a dress that was much less revealing than the one she had worn to the 'wrap' party. This was founced layers of endless numbers of pleats, held together at the waist by a tight, wide leather belt. The dress and the belt were both a startling canary yellow. She wore yellow shoes to match and carried a small yellow handbag. Somewhere in the pleating the bodice was split from neck to waist but the material was so full her nakedness underneath appeared only in the most fleeting of glimpses.

Jason put his cock away, zipped himself up and washed his hands. He said nothing. He hadn't the slightest idea what to say. Being accosted by women while he peed was not an everyday experience for him.

'So you fucked Martha Morris?' Mrs Talbot said flatly. She took a small silver cigarette case from her handbag, took a fat handrolled joint from out of it, and lit it carefully with a gold

Cartier cigarette lighter. She drew deeply on the joint, then blew the smoke out in a straight line.

'What makes you think that?' Jason was not used to discussing his sexual conquests so openly - though what had happened with Martha Morris could hardly be called a conquest.

'She told me. She told me you were very good at it. She's told half the women at this party. They all want to get into your knickers.'

'And what did you tell her in return?'

'Nothing. I'm from New England. Vermont. In Vermont it's considered bad manners to discuss sex. In Hollywood it's *de rigueur*.'

'You can say that again.'

'Did you want me to?'

'No.'

'That's all right then. Not that I didn't agree with her.' Mrs Talbot lent against the vanity unit, her back to the wall of mirrors. He could see her blonde hair reflected in the long mirror that ran the length of the room.

'I've been wanting to talk to you in private.'

'You followed me up here?'

'Yes. Can I tell you something, Jason?'

'Yes.' Jason really wanted to say 'no' and run. He wished he wasn't there. But, by now, he knew Mrs Talbot was not a woman he should offend, not for his sake or for Hanna's which, at the moment, was probably the same thing. He tried to look interested.

'I've never been unfaithful to my husband. By that I mean I have had lots of lovers, but always arranged by him. He's always been there, at least to start with. It was our understanding. He's not a good lover. Never was. So we came to this understanding. Very civilised.' She took a long draw on the joint. 'I, on the other hand, am a very demanding lover. I need special things, as you have seen. I need games. I need to fill my mind with strange ideas.'

'Yes, I saw . . .'

'You don't even know my name, do you?'

'No.'

'My name is Helen.'

'Helen,' he said. It seemed totally inappropriate.

'You make it sound very English.'

'It's a very English name.'

'Yes. I suppose so. In Vermont they adore anything English.'

'So what were you saying?' he prompted, wanting this to end quickly. The bathroom was full of the sickly sweet smell of cannabis.

'Oh yes. I was saying I have a very active imagination.'

'I noticed . . .'

'And it's been working on you. What I could do with you. What I would like to do with you. And that's the problem.'

'Surely not?' he mocked, once again feeling uncomfortably like an object.

'Yes, the problem is that I don't want to have my husband's piggy little eyes watching. I want to be alone. That's what I imagined. And of course, that would mean my being unfaithful to him, well, what I think of as unfaithful, at least.'

'Oh dear,' Jason said sarcastically.

'Do I want to take that risk, I ask myself? If he ever found out he'd dump me so fast I wouldn't feel the ground under my feet. I'd be back at Central Casting in the file marked blondes

162

- and in Hollywood that's a very fat file, believe me.'

'You were an actress?'

'Jason, haven't you learned that by now? Every girl in Hollywood is an actress, it's just that they have to do proper jobs to pay for the acting classes. I was going to be the next Veronica Lake.'

'That's how you met your husband?'

She ignored the question. 'So you see my dilemma?'

'I think I'd better get back . . .'

'It's serious. I thought to myself, is it worth it? Is this beautiful English stud worth losing everything for?'

'Definitely not,' he said with relief.

She dropped the joint into the loo bowl and walked to the bathroom door, her high heels clacking loudly on the marble floor, her hips swaying, swishing the pleats of the dress from side to side. Jason's relief was short-lived. Helen pressed the button in the middle of the door handle that dead-locked the door. She turned back, looking Jason straight in the eyes.

'I'm a slut, you know that, don't you?'

'Look I've got to . . .'

'This won't take long. We have a place at the beach. In a couple of days I'll take you there. I have a special room there . . .' Another special room, like the summerhouse, Jason thought. Hollywood was obviously full of them. ' . . . to cater for my vivid imagination.'

'And what happens if I don't want to come?'

Helen laughed, an odd, brittle sound. 'Don't you want me Jason? Don't you find me attractive? I know you do. You proved it already.'

'What about Hanna?'

Another laugh. 'Hanna gave you to me, remember? I'm sure if I told her you weren't being co-operative . . .'

'So you get what you want,' he said. The smoke of the cannabis was making him feel light-headed. He was sure there was some way, some witty clever way, he could talk himself out of this situation, but his powers of reasoning seemed to be affected by the cannabis.

'Yes, Jason, I get what I want. And I want something on account, as they say . . .'

She was standing with her back to the bathroom door on the white marble step that led through to the bedroom. With Jason on the lower level of the bathroom floor, the step made them virtually the same height.

'And what is that?' he said wearily.

'Come here and kiss me.' She held out her arms. As he walked towards her he had the impression of walking into a Venus fly trap. The arms closed around him as her mouth found his. Her lips felt hard. She kissed him hard, pushing her tongue down between his lips, her hand moving up his spine until it held the back of his neck. She sucked his tongue into her mouth then took it between her teeth as if wanting to tell him she could bite it. His erection stiffened between their bodies.

'Oh Jason, you turn me on . . .' she said, pulling away and looking into his eyes six inches from her face. He hadn't noticed before but her eyes were ice blue, so pale they looked almost grey.

Her hands were on his shoulders, pushing him to his knees. He did not resist. He couldn't resist. He felt high and excited. The soft yellow material of the dress grazed his face. He could smell her musky expensive perfume. As soon as he was down her hands gathered the skirt of the dress at both sides, pulling it up, inching the pleats up over her legs.

Jason watched as the material revealed her creamy flesh. She was not wearing tights. Her thighs were ample, full and soft. The skirt rose tantalisingly slowly.

'Just a taste, Jason, a taste of what is to come . . .'

She bunched the skirt in her fingers, pulling it up as if gathering in a fishing net. Now he could see her thighs and the apex of her sex. She was not wearing knickers either. She raised the skirt higher until she was naked below the waist, her belly flat, the fine pubic hair revealing the runnel of her sex. She spread her legs apart, leaning back against the door.

Not needing to be told what to do, Jason plunged his head forward, kissing and licking at her pubic triangle. He took her pubic hair in his teeth and pulled it back, making her squeal before he worked down, sliding his hands around her thighs for leverage, his tongue in the crease of her sex searching for her clitoris.

Her sex was already wet. She had turned herself on with words. She held the skirt hard against her chest, squeezing her own breasts under the palms of her hands.

Jason found the rigid button of her clitoris with the tip of his tongue. He pressed his fingers into her thighs. The rich musky perfume mixed with the aroma of sex. He worked aggressively, licking upwards so her clitoris was pulled up, stretched up, then released. He was in no mood for subtlety. He felt her react. It was as if her whole body was lifted on the upstroke of his tongue, lifted on to her toes, slumping down again as her clitoris was freed.

She was coming. It was too much for her. He could feel it

and hear it. She was moaning. Her hand left one breast and she jammed her fist into her mouth to try and stop it but she could not prevent some sound. Her clitoris was on fire. His tongue was so hot and hard and cunning. So expert. She felt herself brought up on to tiptoes again as his tongue pushed higher, and then she was over the edge, unable to stop herself, falling down into a black pit of feeling, driven by his relentless tongue and thoughts of what she would do to him when she got him to her cabin at the beach.

Her body shook, like a dog out of water, an involuntary convulsion. Seconds passed, minutes perhaps, before the feelings finally allowed her back into the real world.

Unsteadily Jason got to his feet. She let her skirt fall back over her legs. She caught his arm and pulled him into a kiss, kissing him hungrily, licking her juices from his mouth.

'I'd like to fuck you,' she said, looking at the erection tenting Jason's trousers.

'We both have to get back,' he said. If she'd insisted there was no way he could have stopped her.

'You're right,' she said.

He didn't know whether he was relieved or disappointed.

'I was thinking of what I am going to do to you,' she said. She went over to the mirror and took a small make-up case out of her bag. She rubbed her lips with her finger, then sucked the finger into her mouth.

'I taste good, don't I?'

'You smell good too.'

'Givenchy. I never use anything else.'

'It smells so sexy.'

'That's why I buy it.'

Satisfied that she had repaired any damage to her face Helen unlocked the bathroom door.

'Bye, lover . . . See you in a couple of days,' she said. And then she was gone.

# Chapter Eight

Jason ate some of the Provencal specialties that still lay in abundance on the buffet. The food was delicious and he felt better. The experience in the bathroom had left him feeling feeble-minded, like a pawn in a game he did not understand. The whole thing had a dream-like quality though he knew perfectly well it was real. He could still smell the Givenchy perfume. It seemed to cling to him, to his clothes and his face.

One of the waitresses offered him champagne but he declined. He was intoxicated enough without alcohol.

He looked around for Helen's husband but couldn't see him. He would have expected Hanna to be shepherding him but she was still talking earnestly to the Japanese contingent. Helen was nowhere to he seen either so they must have gone home. Martha Morris had disappeared too.

It was time for the band to transform itself into the mufti of nineties rock, so for the moment there was no music and the balmy night air was filled with the chatter of conversation.

'Hi, hon . . .' Hanna caught his arm. 'Having fun?'

'Great. It's a great party. Must have cost a fortune.'

'The tax man pays.'

'I expected to see Camilla.'

'Oh, she's busy. Working. Who have you met?'

'I saw Martha.'

'Yes. All the same old faces. Sad, really.'

'Sad?'

'It's a vicious circle. They come here. I go there . . .'

'How's George Mason?'

'I had him taken home. Pissed as usual. If he wasn't so old he'd die young.'

'Is he always like that?'

'Always. As long as I've known him.'

'How did he manage to direct all those films?'

'I told you, he points the cameras. I get him a good crew and a good cast. It's all done by mirrors . . . You've got a lot to learn about this business, Jason . . .'

Hanna seemed relaxed and happy. They sat at a table and chatted amiably about the film business. Jason felt increasingly reassured that what she had told him in the bedroom was the truth.

By the time the music re-started and the more energetic dancing got underway Jason's mood was edging on the euphoric. While Hanna went to see off a couple of the guests who had to leave, Jason introduced himself to one or two people and was asked about England, the weather, the theatre, and the studios. He danced a couple of times, and finding himself out of breath, made a mental note to use the house gym tomorrow as it had been some days since he'd worked out.

Gradually people began to drift away. The rock band played slow tempo numbers and fewer and fewer couples smooched around. The car jockeys, included in the package provided by Didier Paparemborde, brought a series of sleek, expensive, exclusively foreign, cars around to the front door to be driven away by their owners, while a series of chauffeurs arrived with the limousines – Cadillacs, Mercedes and Rolls Royces – to take away those who never drove themselves.

The waitresses began to clear up, ferrying plates and glasses back into the mobile kitchen. The band called it a day too and started to pack up their equipment. Jason looked around for Hanna. He found her in the swimming pool. The lilies and candles had all drifted to one corner and Hanna was stroking lazily up the opposite side in her white swimsuit. That was a good sign, he thought. Swimming always had a beneficial effect on Hanna's mood.

'Come on in,' she shouted when she saw him.

'Good idea.' It was. The night was still balmy, whether because of the heaters hidden in the bushes, or naturally he did not know. He loped upstairs and changed into the swimming trunks they had bought on Rodeo Drive. They were little more than a black triangle of Lycra covering his genitals and held in place by thin elasticated thongs.

Downstairs he ran across the terrace and took a flying dive into the pool. He swam straight up to Hanna, wrapped his arm around her waist and kissed her mouth. They began to sink, but she kissed him back, wriggling her body against his. They bumped along the bottom of the pool, holding their breath. Then, the need to breathe overcoming their passion, they exploded apart and raced to the surface, shooting from the water gasping and gulping down air.

They swam lazily, then raced. Hanna won, her ease in the water more than a match for Jason's power.

Eventually they climbed out and dried themselves on big white towels under the stars. A few guests still sat around, mostly couples gazing earnestly into each other's eyes.

'Let's go inside . . .' Jason said eagerly.

'I need to talk to you first . . .' Hanna replied.

'We can talk upstairs . . .' Jason took her hand. She tried to resist but he pulled her through the terrace doors into the living room. There he stopped in his tracks. Sitting on the far side of the room, on the small sofa where they had been when he first met them, were Harriet Teitelbaum and Cynthia.

Jason knew at once what Hanna wanted to talk about. His heart fell.

'I told you I need to talk,' Hanna said, her voice hard and unemotional.

'The answer is no.' He looked over at the two women. Cynthia smiled at him, Harry stared expressionless. They were too far away to hear the conversation.

'Let me finish . . .'

'Hanna, I thought we had this out . . .'

'Listen. Talbot's wobbling on my film . . . he may pull out. If I could tell him Harry would come in with half the money then he'd commit definitely. It's as simple as that. I get my film, you get the part. We're all happy.'

'The part?'

'Jason, I know you now. I mean, I have to do a screen test for the studio but that's just a formality. You'll get the part.'

'As long as I do what?'

'She's got the hots for you, Jason. She came right out with it in front of Martha.'

'What about me? Don't I get a say?'

'What'll it cost? Eh? A little harmless fun? You'll enjoy it.'

'With her? She looks like a man.'

Hanna sat down in a straight-backed dining chair and pulled Jason down to sit in the chair besides her.

'OK. It's your choice, Jason. I'm asking you to do me a small favour.'

'Small!'

'Shut up. I like you, Jason. But you have to help me.'

'Or else?'

'Exactly.'

'Or else what?'

'Or else, Jason, you will never work in any picture of mine. Nor any picture, period. This is a very small world. Everyone who was anyone in Hollywood was here tonight. I've only got to say the word and you're finished. Is that clear enough?'

She paused to let the threat sink in. Jason said nothing.

'I don't want to do that. I like you. I like you a lot. Help me, Jason, and I'll help you. I could make you a star . . .'

If his mood hadn't been so bleak Jason would have laughed at this last remark.

Harriet Teitelbaum had lost patience. She was not accustomed to being kept waiting. Her eyes had never left Jason's body. Though she couldn't hear what Hanna was saying she knew what was being negotiated. And she knew what she wanted. It was the ultimate satisfaction of her life, of her position, that she inevitably got what she wanted. That was Hollywood. So many people, so much competition. People would do anything for an edge, to get ahead, to stick their necks out in front.

Harry got up from the sofa and walked across the room. Cynthia trailed in her wake.

'No problems, I hope,' she said to Hanna.

'He's big, isn't he. Look at those muscles.' Cynthia said.

'Is there any problem, Jason?' Hanna asked pointedly.

Decision time. Jason stood up, his strong body naked but for the triangle of black nylon over his belly. Cynthia extended her hand to touch his chest, rather like someone wanting to touch a strange, exotic, and perhaps dangerous animal for the first time. In his mind there were a thousand things he wanted to say to Hanna, a thousand rebukes, a thousand 'how dare yous'. He wanted to go upstairs, call a cab, wait at the airport for the next plane out of this crazy city. But against every phrase, against every urge to damn the lot of them, he saw a mental picture of the ornate frontage of Graumann's Chinese Theatre on Hollywood Boulevard lit up with neon announcing, 'JASON MACIVER in a Hanna Silverstein production of . . .'

'No,' he said flatly, answering Hanna's question. 'No problem.'

Hanna didn't look at him again, not directly. She went over to the bar and poured two drinks.

Harry's hand tried to circle his bicep but was not big enough. It was the gesture of someone who had just bought a new horse, and was trying to gauge how powerful it really was. Harry was short and stout though not fat. Her face had a slightly oriental slant, her cheeks rather chubby, her eyes and mouth elongated, her nose small and unobtrusive. It was impossible to tell, under the suit, what her body was like, but her chest was clearly flat.

Drink this,' Hanna said, handing Jason a glass.

'I don't want anything else to drink,' he said.

'Jason, trust me. Drink it.'

Actually she was right. He did need a drink. He gulped back

the golden liquid in the glass and discovered it was brandy. It tasted sour and unpleasant, though. Despite the taste he finished the glass.

He smiled to himself. He had just found something out about his character. Before, he had never known how much he really wanted to succeed in his profession. Well, now he knew exactly. He obviously wanted to succeed very much.

It was not like feeling drunk. He could walk in a straight line, he could balance perfectly. It was just that nothing was quite in focus. Everything seemed far away, like looking through the wrong end of a pair of binoculars.

It had started as he'd walked through into the hall on his way upstairs to put on some clothes. The three women had followed him. Hanna had opened the front door. Beyond it he could see a black Cadillac outside on the driveway, its rear passenger door held open by a uniformed blonde chauffeuse, her grey suit revealing long slender legs perched on extravagantly high heels. He could see into the interior of the car, the black leather seats, the dark wool rugs, the fake wood divider between driver and passenger, all lit by the overhead lamp set in the roof lining.

He'd got to the bottom of the curving staircase and looked up. Instead of a single flight of stairs to the first floor landing, there had been a huge, endless staircase, hundreds of steps, leading up into the clear star-lit night sky. He couldn't possibly climb that many stairs.

'There's too many,' he said.

'Sure there are,' Harry said. She took his arm by the wrist. He'd expected her hand to feel hard, like a man's hand, but it didn't. It was soft, incredibly soft. It didn't feel like a hand at all. And his wrist was so sensitive suddenly. Not only sensitive but sexy. How could he feel like this, he was getting an erection, and she was only touching his wrist?

'Come with me, Jason,' Harry said firmly.

'Come with us,' Cynthia giggled.

He wanted to tell them he couldn't go anywhere without his clothes. Instead he said, 'That feels so good.'

His erection had nosed out of the front of the miniscule swimming trunks. He tried to cover it with his hand. Cynthia giggled again.

Harry led him past Hanna at the front door. There was a look in her eyes he didn't understand. She looked sad. Had Harry ever touched her like this, he wondered. He put out his hand to grasp her wrist. Perhaps her wrist was as sensitive as his was now. They'd never tried that. But as he groped around he realised he couldn't reach. She was too far away. Never mind. He didn't mind. He didn't mind anything.

They were man-handling him into the car. Cynthia had got in first and was pulling him, while Harry pushed from behind. He could feel her hand on his rump. It was hot. He could feel his flesh react, it was as though she were touching his cock. Every part of his body was alive. He felt so sexy.

But he couldn't get into the car in just his swimming trunks. Not these swimming trunks. He tried to turn round. Hanna stood by the car door.

'No, Jason, you've got to go.'

'I have to change,' he said.

Then he was sitting in the big leather seat and the car was driving on a main road. Had they pushed him back in? He hadn't felt the car start. Cynthia was sitting on the jump seat facing him. He could see the silk panel of her panties stretched over her sex. He could see her small breasts under the transparent dress. Her nipples were out of all proportion to the breast they surmounted. They were big and bulbous.

'I can see you,' he said.

His erection still poked out of the top of the trunks. The whole of his glans was exposed.

'I can see you too,' Cynthia said.

'No . . .' he put his hand over his cock.

'Are your nipples sensitive, Jason?' Harry, who was sitting beside him, asked.

'Hanna told you . . .' He sounded like a schoolboy whose best friend had betrayed the secret location of their tree house to an arch enemy.

Harry licked the tip of her finger with her tongue, wetting it with saliva, then circled it around Jason's nipple, the saliva making the contact slick and frictionless.

'Very sensitive, aren't they?' she said. It was obvious. Jason's body quivered.

'Do you want to see my cock?' he said.

'Yes.'

He pulled his hand away. 'Shall I take my knickers off? They're uncomfortable . . .'

'Yes. You take them off.'

But he couldn't. He couldn't find the narrow thong of black at his waist. All he could feel was his own flesh. But that felt good. He stroked it. Oh, how good that felt.

'That's better,' Harry said.

'Much better.' Cynthia was holding his black trunks up in

front of him. How had she done that? He covered his cock with both his hands.

'Come on, let me see it . . .' Harry said.

'Don't touch it.'

'I won't.'

He took his hands away, relaxing in the big bucket seat, pushing his cock up so they could see it. He looked at it himself. It was very hard. He saw Harry looking at it too.

Cynthia knelt on the deep pile wood carpet in front of him.

'It's big . . .' she said.

'Yes.'

'We can't take you in like this, can we? You have to wear something,' Harry explained.

'I can't go in like this,' Jason agreed earnestly. He had no idea where 'in', might be nor did he care. What he really wanted to do was wank. He didn't think he'd ever felt so sensitive in his entire life. Cynthia's dress was brushing against his knee. That feeling alone was making him shudder with pleasure. The material felt so silky, so soft.

Harry had something in her hand. Jason panicked. She had murdered the President of the United States and cut off his head. Now she was showing it to him.

'No . . .' he screamed.

'Sh . . . It's only a mask. A party mask. If you're going to a party you have to have a mask, don't you?'

'Of course,' Jason said, relaxing again. Did they think he was stupid? Harry pulled the mask down over his head. There was a hole for his mouth and his eyes.

He looked down at Cynthia. She was holding a shiny metal chain. He was confused again. It was Hanna's chain, the one she had used on him that first night. What were they doing with it?

'What are you doing with it?'

'You have to be properly dressed,' Harry said.

'Open your legs up . . .' Cynthia said. It wasn't Hanna's chain. It was much longer. Delicately Cynthia reached forward and looped the chain under his balls and around the stem of his cock. She snapped a tiny padlock in place holding the chain tight around his erection. He thought he was going to come with the feeling while she fixed the chain. Her hands brushed his cock. It had never felt like this.

There was still a length of chain in Cynthia's hand. It was anchored to the chain around his cock.

'This is for the nipples,' Cynthia said, showing him the clips identical to the ones Hanna had used.

'I know that.' He knew that.

She manoeuvred the clips over his nipples and opened the little serrated jaws, allowing them to sink into his corrugated flesh both at the same time. This time he thought he had come. Pleasure coursed through his body, every nerve enraptured. He closed his eyes to wallow in the ecstasy.

When he opened them again the car was going steeply down hill, down a ramp and into a tunnel, except the tunnel soon widened into a huge dark empty cavern. To Jason the underground car park looked like a vast dark cave hewn from rock. The car stopped at the lift shaft.

Jason looked down at his body, expecting to see a trail of spunk. Instead he saw his cock, hard and erect. From the circle of chain padlocked tightly around it, another chain was loosely connected to the middle of the loop of links that lay across his chest joining the two nipple clips.

'Don't you look pretty?' Cynthia said.

'Are you awake again now?' Harry asked.

'I haven't been asleep,' he said angrily.

The passenger door opened. The blonde chauffeuse stood holding it. Her long legs were encased in the sheerest nylon Jason had ever seen.

'Do you like my cock?' Jason asked her.

'Very much, sir,' she said.

'I'd like to fuck you.'

'I'd like that very much, sir,' she replied.

Suddenly he was standing outside the car. He moved to kiss the object of his affections but she moved aside.

'Why wouldn't you let me kiss you?' he said.

'Later, perhaps,' she said. He watched as she got back into the car.

'Don't go.'

'This way,' Harry said.

'Where are you taking me?'

'Home.' Cynthia said.

'To a party.'

'That's right.'

Then he was standing in the lift, its metal walls cold against his back. He looked at the chains. He felt deliciously like a hand was gripping his cock and two little mouths sucking permanently at his nipples.

'Going up,' Cynthia said. The lift had only one button. She pressed it. Jason was sure the lift was going down.

The lift doors opened. Harry twisted Jason's mask around, effectively blindfolding him.

'It's dark here,' he said.

'Yes, but I know the way.'

Jason felt a hand pulling him forward. He thought he could hear voices, different voices, chattering voices, party voices, but they were faint and soon faded away. He decided he wanted to fuck Cynthia if he couldn't fuck the chauffeuse. He had to fuck someone. She was not beautiful. Not like Camilla. But she was sexy, dirty sexy, the sort of girl at school everyone talked about and did dirty things with. As soon as they switched the lights on he'd tell her. Harry could watch. He wouldn't mind that. He wouldn't mind anything as long as he fucked someone.

A hand stopped him in his tracks. Two hands held him from the back by the shoulders. He heard a voice, but this time a solo voice. It was too far away for him to hear what it was saying. He thought he heard music, music that sounded like an anthem. Was it the American anthem? It didn't last long.

The mask was pulled round so he could see again. The hands on his shoulders pushed him forward.

As far as he could tell he was in a black room. The only furniture was a double bed covered in a white sheet. On the bed Cynthia lay naked. Well, that was a relief, he wasn't going to have to ask to fuck her, he thought. There were several spotlights trained on the bed from the ceiling. The room had a huge window, almost the whole of one wall, but it had no curtains and beyond, outside the glass there was no view of anything but blackness. That was logical, he reasoned, it was night time. It was probably desert out there, with no street lights. They were in the desert. That was why it was hot. The room was very hot.

'Mr President . . .' Cynthia said. She was lying on her back with her legs open and her knees bent. He had never seen such a bush of pubic hair. It was thick and wiry and jet black. But it had been trimmed savagely. Instead of the normal triangle on her belly there was a thin oval shape. Over her sex too it was cut back so it covered only the very edges of her labia.

'You're not a natural blonde,' he said. He could have sworn he heard laughter. Someone must be having a party. Where was the party they'd promised him?

'Are you going to fuck me, Mr President?' she asked. 'I need it. I really need it. My cunny aches for it.'

'Fuck . . .' he was confused again.

'Fuck. You do know how to?'

More imagined laughter from the imagined party.

He knelt on the bed, between her open legs. This was going to be difficult, he thought. He had never felt so excited. He was bound to come immediately he thought. Or did he say it out loud?

'I'll come,' he heard himself say that.

'That's what I want.'

He inched forward feeling his cock brush against her pubic hair. He closed his eyes with pleasure.

'I've come,' he said.

'No you haven't. You're going to come inside me.'

Oh yes please, he thought or said, or both.

He leant forward and suddenly felt his cock sucked inside her, right up to the hilt. His chest rested against hers, instantly making the nipple clips bite more deeply. Pleasure rushed through him again, like a wave breaking on the shore.

'What do you want?' Cynthia said into his ear. She pushed

her tongue right inside his ear. He shuddered. More exquisite pleasure.

'Anything,' he said, squirming against her body.

'Shall I have you whipped while you're fucking me, Mr President?'

He was so stupid. Why hadn't he thought of that? His arse wanted it, needed it. It felt exposed sticking up in the air. It needed whipping. Like he'd whipped Camilla. Where was Camilla? Perhaps she'd be at this other party.

Cynthia held his face in both her hands and kissed him on the mouth as the first blow struck. He tried to look round but she wouldn't let him turn his face away from her. She held it tight. She was strong. He'd never been whipped before. The second blaze of fire hit his buttocks. His cock jerked in her cunt. He felt her spasm in return.

Why hadn't he come? Had he dreamt of being whipped? Was that his fantasy? He couldn't remember. It felt good, hot, sexy. He wanted to see who was doing it to him, but Cynthia wouldn't let him.

'I'm coming,' he said.

Her body felt so thin and fragile and vulnerable. Not like Hanna's, all hard and bony, not like Martha's, spongy and soft, not like Helen's, not like Camilla's. Oh Camilla. Camilla, who is the most beautiful of them all. Mirror, mirror on the wall. He saw her face in the big window, behind the big window.

'I'm coming,' he said again as the whip stroked his arse.

'You can't,' Cynthia said.

The whipping had stopped. His arse was sore and burning. His cock felt so erect he thought it would burst, not with spunk, but with blood, just swell up and burst.

Of course he could come. He thrust into her violently, wanting to prove her wrong, feeling the heat across his buttocks, red welts of heat, striped across his arse. So good. So hot. Of course he could come. He rammed up into her. Her hands, cool, long fingers, found his buttocks. They caressed the welts. That would do it. That was the final straw, cool hands on radiant heat. He would come, flood her with his spunk. On her hands alone, that feeling alone.

He felt her come. Her body convulsed under him. He ignored it, ramming on and on. He was on the brink, the very brink but that was as far as he could drive himself. No further. Not over. Just up to. He felt his nipples with their little sucking mouths, he felt her hands on his arse, felt his balls tied in a chain. Sensation everywhere but it didn't make him come. He thought of Camilla. He thought of those black French knickers being pulled up her long thighs in the bathroom of the hotel in London. He felt himself surging into Cynthia's wet, silky, clinging cunt. He came closer and closer to the brink. But not over it.

He stopped thrusting.

'Sh . . .' Cynthia whispered. 'It's the drug. It'll wear off.' She had whispered right into his ear so no one else could hear. She felt sorry for him.

'Ready?' It was Harry's voice, strong and powerful.

'He's ready,' Cynthia said.

'I'm ready,' Jason agreed weakly, not knowing what for.

Harry was naked. Her body was surprisingly attractive. She was no great beauty but her short legs were firm, her belly only slightly plump and her breasts tiny but rounded. This time Cynthia did not stop Jason looking round.

'Where have you been?' he asked. Harry had the smallest

nipples he thought he'd ever seen, no bigger than pin-pricks, and a raw pink in colour. He could not see her cunt. Instead it looked as though she had a cock, a black leather cock.

Jason suddenly felt tired, he wanted to sleep. He wanted to roll over and go to sleep. He couldn't keep his eyes open.

She was a man. That's why she wore a suit, because she was really a man. Everyone was wrong. He'd tell Hanna. He'd tell Martha. He'd explain. She was a man with tits. Or was it all a dream? Was he already asleep?

Harry knelt on the bed behind them. He felt Cynthia's hands on his buttocks, spreading them apart.

'I can't come,' he said, or thought he said.

'I know,' Harry's voice was husky. 'I'm going to help you.'

'I can't stay awake.'

Something hard was nudging between the cheeks of his arse.

'I'll make you come.' Harry said.

'I want to sleep.'

Jason closed his eyes. He felt warm and comfortable. His body was full of pleasure. He started to dream the moment he was asleep. It was a confusing dream, like dreams can be. Harry was a woman with a cock. A leather cock strapped on by thick black straps. She was using it on Jason. He watched himself from somewhere high above as she did it.

Then Jason fucked Harry, hard and fast. Buggered her too, he thought. And Cynthia was still there. He couldn't tell who he was fucking, it was that sort of dream. He wasn't surprised that Camilla was in the dream too. Camilla fucked him, sitting on top of him. It was Camilla that got him over the brink. He wasn't surprised he came in his dream either. It was bound to be a wet dream after all he'd been through. A big wet dream ending between Camilla's shaven sex.

He dreamt for a long time after that. He dreamt the window wasn't a window at all. He dreamt there were rows of seats behind it and a camera. What a dream. What a crazy dream. All the time he was dreaming he knew it was a dream. He knew he was in bed, in that huge bed in Hanna's house.

He dreamt he was hard again. Then it all faded into shadows. He remembered dreaming that the chains were taken off, the little padlock opened with a little key.

He remembered the lift. 'Going down,' someone said. The lift went up.

The chauffeuse was waiting. Back in the car. His nipples were sore, and his cock and his arse, where he'd dreamt it had been whipped and fucked. But not for one second did he mind in his dream. It was a dream of pure pleasure . . . a dream of life. When he opened his eyes, just once to reassure himself, he was lying in Hanna's bed, so he knew he had been right and dreamt a dream of dreaming.

# Chapter Nine

The light woke him. The sun had cleared the shade of the trees and now streamed in through the white curtains of the bedroom windows. Jason moved his head away from it and immediately felt as though he had been hit in the head with a sledgehammer. His head throbbed with vicious pain.

'Eh . . .' he moaned and wished he hadn't. The noise reverberated through the room and came back into his ears doubling the pain.

Very slowly he raised himself from the pillow. He was alone in the big bed, which hardly surprised him. He had woken alone every morning. He looked at his watch as soon as he'd worked out how to focus his eyes without increasing the pain. It was twelve o'clock. How could it be so late? That was another mistake. The concentrated effort of thinking just produced another pulsating cloud of pain.

Gingerly he walked into the bathroom, every step an exercise in how delicately he could move without jarring his head. In the bathroom cabinet he found aspirin and took four.

He looked at his face in the mirror. There were dark bags under his eyes, and despite the Californian sun on his face, he looked pale. He examined his nipples. Two crescents of tiny little bruises were cut into each. He looked over his shoulder –

another mistake, another cloud of pain – and saw deep red marks crossing his buttocks, four or five at least, in varying shades of red, from light pink to deep vermilion.

It had not been a dream. Anger surged up in him, joined the headache and made matters worse. He sat down on the loo. His arse felt sore but it was not painful. Gradually the aspirin took effect. The banging in his head subsided to a dull ache and he could think clearly without provoking further torture.

He had been drugged, given something that had produced the dream-like quality and his euphoria. He couldn't remember much of what had happened. He remembered riding in the car, he remembered making love to Cynthia and being beaten. He remembered the chains they had attached to his body but that was about it. He hadn't the slightest idea of how he had got back to the house and ended up naked in bed. He had vague flashes and images beyond that but trying to bring them to life only resuscitated the throbbing in his head. It didn't matter anyway, enough was enough.

Hanna had used him. Hanna had given him his last drink. He clearly remembered that. She had drugged him.

Jason showered, treating himself with infinite care. He pulled on a pair of slacks and a shirt.

Downstairs Maria was working in the kitchen.

'Morning, sir,' she said cheerily. 'You look like you enjoy the party a little bit too much.' Outside the caterers were taking away their napery, the tables and chairs, and dismantling the strings of lights in the garden. The pool man was emptying the pool of lilies and candle-holders. 'I cook you a nice breakfast, then you feel better, yes?'

'Yes.' He realised he was very hungry. 'I'm starving.' The headache had diminished to a dull pounding. It had moved from over both his eyes to the back of his head. Any sudden movement brought it swiftly to the fore again. Food would make him feel better.

In minutes Maria had prepared a plate of scrambled eggs, grilled tomatoes and ham, with wholewheat toast which he devoured rapidly. He drank orange juice and a whole pot of steaming black coffee and poured maple syrup over the thick pancakes Maria presented him with as she took his first plate away.

He felt better. He felt well enough to allow anger to resurface.

'Where's Hanna?'

'Ms Hanna gone to the studio.'

'What time did she leave?'

'Early. Always been the same with her. No matter how late she's going to bed, always up early.'

'And no matter how much she's drunk,' Jason said, almost to himself.

Maria looked at him with her head cocked to one side. 'I like you, Mr Jason,' she said. It was as though she was about to say something else, then decided against it. She went back to her washing up.

Jason finished all the pancakes. He was going to drive out to the studios and confront Hanna. He actually had no idea what he was going to say. He would play it by ear, he decided. His inclination was to rush in like a bull in a china shop and tell her exactly what he thought of the way he had been treated, the way she had used him.

On the other hand, what had happened was over, it was past.

If she'd told him the truth last night, if she was going to arrange the screen test, if that was just a formality, then, what was the point in making a fuss? He would make it clear to her that he was not prepared to be used again, never to be passed around among her friends, but to rant and rave at her would be pointless. Not if he were going to get the part.

He went to the garage, took the keys of the Mercedes 600SL off the board and got into its plush leather interior. He took the map from the glove compartment and studied it. Suddenly an image flashed into his mind, an image of Camilla, naked but for a pair of thigh-length leather boots. She was bent over the bed facing him and Harriet Teitelbaum was standing behind her. He tried to concentrate but the memory faded as rapidly as it had arrived. That must have been a dream. Camilla hadn't been there, in that strange room. He must have dreamt it when he got back home, imposing his dream-like reality on real dreams. In the state he had been in it wasn't surprising.

With the map open on the passenger seat Jason drove up to Burbank. Apart from missing his turning on the five-lane freeway and having to make an eight-mile detour to the next exit, he found his way with little trouble. He pulled the car up to the large security barrier in front of the studio entrance.

'Hanna Silverstein,' he said to the guard, lowering the window of the Mercedes at the touch of a button.

'You got an appointment, bud?' The guard was black and incredibly tall. He looked as though he played basketball for the Los Angeles Lakers.

'No, but she'll see me . . .'

'All the others got appointments.'

'What others?'

'You're an actor, right. With that accent you have to be an actor.'

'Right.'

'Your name?'

'Jason MacIver.'

'There's no MacIver on my list.' He was consulting his clipboard.

'Look, this is Ms Silverstein's car. Would you just ring her office?'

'Sure thing, bud. Just wait one. More than my job's worth to let you in without a say-so. You dig that?'

'Of course.'

The guard loped back into his glass-fronted booth and punched a number into the telephone. Jason could see his lips moving but could not hear what he said. He put the phone down and formed an 'o' with his thumb and forefinger. The barrier in front of the Mercedes went up like a railway signal.

'Which way?' Jason shouted.

The guard came out of the booth again. 'Straight down. Last block. Big sign, you can't miss it.'

'Thanks.'

Jason gunned the big engine and drove carefully between the huge sound stages. Unlike in the numerous films he'd seen about Hollywood there was very little activity, no extras in extravagant costumes roaming the lot, no flats being carried, no animals waiting for their scenes. There were one or two pieces of plaster work stacked outside the main dock doors, a Doric column, a scaled down version of a suspension bridge, and several rusting scene weights, but apart from these there was little clue to what went on in the vast buildings he was driving past.

The guard was right. It was impossible to miss Hanna's office. A large white sign with blue letters two foot high read: SILVERSTEIN PRODUCTIONS INC.

Jason parked the car and walked through the double glass doors into a luxurious reception area. The carpet was thick, the chairs modern and black leather, the reception desk a creation of chrome and glass. It was impossible not to be impressed. The reception area delivered the message it was designed to deliver: Silverstein Productions was a prestige company, Hollywood's finest.

To Jason's surprise the twenty or so leather chairs and sofas were all occupied, and their occupants were all men the same age as him. Not only that, they were all slim, fit looking, and all with various shades of blond hair. They were all reading scripts in orange bindings.

'Can I help you?' the petite brunette behind the reception desk asked.

'Jason MacIver,' he replied.

She consulted a file on the desk. 'I don't have a Jason MacIver down here. Did the gate let you in?'

'Of course they did. Just tell Hanna I'm here,' he snapped. A realisation was beginning to dawn on him. What had the taxi driver told him?

One of the men laid his orange script down on a coffee table and closed his eyes, his lips moving silently as though he were running through the words in his mind to try and memorise them. The front of the binder had a window cut in the orange paper to reveal the title of the script typed on the page underneath. Jason snatched it up. THE CASTING COUCH it read in neat block capitals. THE CASTING COUCH!

'Hey . . .' the young actor protested, opening his eyes.

THE CASTING COUCH! 'You're here to audition for this, right?' Jason said angrily.

'Yah. We all are.'

'Right.'

The script still in his hand, Jason tore past the receptionist and through the swing doors behind her.

'You can't . . .' she shouted, coming after him.

'Hanna! Hanna!' he shouted in the corridor behind the doors.

He threw open the first door he came to. In a small almost empty office George Mason sat behind a table. A young blond actor sat in front of him reading from another orange bound script.

'Sorry,' George said politely, 'I haven't finished yet.'

Jason had never seen him sober. He looked younger, like the publicity photos of him. He looked, for the first time, like a man capable of producing award-winning films.

Slamming the door Jason charged down the corridor again. The brunette receptionist had caught up with him as he opened the next door.

Hanna sat behind a large desk. The office was enormous, a wall of books and scripts to the left, a picture window looking out on the back lot to the right. There were racks of videos, and more expensive modern furniture including a large sofa in white raw silk very like the ones in her bedroom. Another blond actor sat in a chair in front of her desk, another orange script open in his hands.

'I tried to stop him,' the receptionist said.

'I think we should talk, don't you?' Jason said, his steely blue eyes levelled at Hanna, their fury obvious.

'Is there a problem?' she said coolly, sitting back in her leather desk chair.

'You know there is.'

She lent forward slowly and looked at the actor in front of her. 'Chuck, would you mind excusing us for a second? I won't keep you long.'

'Sure thing,' he said, getting up. He looked at Jason with an expression of puzzlement and walked passed the receptionist, who also decided she was no longer required.

'Good morning . . . oh no, it's afternoon,' Hanna said. She tilted back in her chair again. As usual she was wearing white, a simple white blouse and skirt. As usual it was adorned with gold jewellery, a brooch in the shape of a primitive representation of the sun.

'This is a surprise.'

'I bet it is.'

'What are you so mad about?'

'Apart from last night?'

'Don't tell me you didn't have a good time? Harry's very imaginative, I've heard. Unfortunately she's never shown much interest in me . . .'

'You drugged me.'

'And you enjoyed every minute . . .'

'That's not the point.'

'I think it is.'

'And what's going on here, then?'

'I'd have thought that was obvious. We're auditioning.'

'For my part?'

'Of course for your part.' Hanna's voice betrayed no emotion.

'You bitch.'

'Don't call me a bitch.'

'You fucking bitch . . . You had no intention of ever having me in this film, did you? You just brought me here to fuck me and use me. You've used me with the Talbots, with Harry . . .'

'Have I?' Hanna remained calm.

'And now you're auditioning behind my back. And there's suddenly a script. Every time I asked to see this . . .' he waved the orange script in his hand, 'it was being rewritten.' He slammed the script down on her desk.

'Calm down.'

'Don't tell me to calm down. How dare you treat me like this? Just because I didn't know any better . . .'

'Haven't you forgotten something?' Hanna said in the tone of someone trying to explain to a five-year-old.

'What? That I'm an idiot?'

'That you're English.'

'What's that got to do with anything?'

'You need a work permit to work in the States. In order to get you a work permit we have to prove to the Immigration Service that we couldn't find an American actor to play the part. This little charade that George and I are going through is for your benefit, Jason. We've got every blond twenty-year-old in Hollywood. All carefully noted. If the Immigration Service ask we can tell them we tried . . . and failed.'

'Why didn't you show me the script?' Jason felt the wind being taken from his sails.

'I told you last night the rewrites were in. This is straight from the printers. They were waiting for me this morning.'

'Oh.' Jason felt stupid.

'Yes, oh.'

Neither spoke.

'You drugged me,' Jason said feebly.

'I asked you to do me a favour, you agreed.'

If all she said was true, and it looked as though it was, Jason had made a fool of himself, a complete fool. He wished the ground would open and swallow him up. He knew he needed a work permit. It looked as though she was genuinely trying to get him the part.

'How did you get here?' she asked.

'In the Mercedes.'

'Drive it home. Wait for me there. I'll be two hours,' she lied.

'I'm sorry, I just . . . I'm really sorry, Hanna.'

'We'll talk about it later. Go.'

'Can I take a script?'

'Sure. Just go.'

She didn't smile. She rocked back in the chair and closed her eyes as if wishing he wasn't there. She got her wish.

He sat in the Mercedes without starting the engine. He had been an idiot. He had jumped to all the wrong conclusions. He should have known better. He had rushed in and assumed the worst. But was it surprising? Hanna might be playing out an elaborate charade for the Immigration Service's benefit but she could hardly expect to stand on the moral high ground after the way she had used him with the Talbots and Harriet Teitelbaum. She had to admit she'd used him.

In Jason's eyes that made them equal. He'd blundered in and called her a bitch and she'd passed him around like a super-animated stud. That was equal. When she got home that's what he'd tell her. They were equal now. They could start again.

He would make her laugh about it. He'd tell her all the gory details – those he could remember – of last night's proceedings and show her his scars. He'd take her to bed. Perhaps she'd like to be taken down to the summerhouse? Whatever she wanted him to do he'd do. He'd fuck her until she moaned for mercy, until she admitted they had both behaved equally badly.

Meantime he would read the script and start to learn his part. He wanted to be word-perfect for the screen test.

Putting the Mercedes into gear he drove out of the studios and back down to Beverly Hills. It was hot and he stopped to wind the soft top down. Electric motors stowed it away neatly in a few seconds. The wind in his hair made him feel better. His headache had gone completely. He felt extremely chipper to think of Hanna going to all that trouble for his benefit. Not concentrating on the route he got lost. It took him over an hour to get back to the house.

As he drove up the driveway a large van was blocking the turn-off to the garage complex. He parked the car behind it and got out. The van's logo was emblazoned on its side panels: BEVERLY HILLS SECURITY CONSULTANTS. Jason went round to the driver's door.

'Excuse me, can you move over? I want to get to the garages,' he said politely.

'English, right?' the uniformed security guard said. He was big, fat and ugly with a face like a squashed tomato, red and spotted. He got out of the van. Another guard, with the same build and a face that looked as though he had spent too many nights in a boxing ring, came round to join him. Both wore leather belts hanging around their bellies. Attached to the belts were long truncheons, handcuffs and holstered guns.

'I just have to . . .' Jason was about to explain again.

'Keys.'

'Sorry?'

'Car keys.'

'In the car. Look . . .'

The ex-boxer looked into the Mercedes and extracted the keys from the ignition. The engine died.

'Clothes.'

'What?'

'Oh, sorry. Better read this.' He handed Jason a note, a single sheet of paper with the security firm's logo on the top. It had been folded once down the middle.

Jason opened it. Typed neatly in capital letters were ten words: NOBODY TALKS TO ME LIKE THAT. GET LOST. HANNA SILVERSTEIN.

'Clothes,' the guard repeated, seeing Jason had read the message.

'What clothes?' Jason was dazed.

'We got orders to take your clothes. Don't make it difficult. There ain't no percentage in you getting difficult.'

'Here.' The ex-boxer reached into the van and pulled out Jason's briefcase and the jeans and shirt he'd travelled in. They were clean.

'Now get those clothes off.'

'Here?'

'Where else? You ain't allowed in the house.'

'I don't believe this.'

'Believe it. You do it. Or we do it for you.'

'Christ . . .'

Jason saw no choice. He stripped off his shirt and put on the one held out by the guard. He pulled off his trousers.

'You want the pants?' They had been bought on Rodeo Drive too.

'Keep 'em,' the ex-boxer said.

'Who's a lucky boy,' tomato-face jeered.

As Jason pulled on his jeans he saw Maria watching from the upstairs window. Her face looked sad.

Jason put his shoes back on. They were his. He checked the briefcase. It had everything he'd brought with him including his toothbrush. It wasn't much.

'Script?' tomato-face asked.

'In the car.'

The ex-boxer checked and nodded that it was.

'OK. We're all done here. We just have to show you off the premises.'

The guard took Jason's arm. He shook it off. 'It's all right, I'm going.'

'Do yourself a favour, son. Don't come back. Final is final. The cops in Beverly Hills shoot intruders first and ask questions later, got it?'

Jason didn't reply. He walked past the Mercedes and down the driveway. The guards followed him until he was out on the wide pavement lined with trees. They stood by the gate and watched as he trudged up the wide street, past the huge mansions, his briefcase in his hand.

# Chapter Ten

There were no cruising taxis in Los Angeles and besides Jason had no money. The only money he had was the twenty-five pounds in sterling he had had in his wallet the morning Camilla picked him up. He hadn't needed to think about money in Los Angeles. Everything had been paid for.

He looked at his watch. It was coming up to two o'clock. The first thing he needed to do was get change for the phone. Then at least he could call his agent, call Martha Morris, call somebody. He had no idea where the nearest bank was but there must be a bank on Sunset Strip and he knew how to get there on foot without a map.

It took him an hour in the hot sun to walk down to Sunset. It took him another fifteen minutes to find a bank. Fortunately they were still open. He changed his money into dollars and got quarters for the phone.

Outside in the heat again he found a pay-phone a little way from the bank. He dialled the number for Hammerstein and Cohen.

'Who's calling?' the receptionist asked.

'Jason MacIver.'

'Hold the line, please.' There was a pause. 'Mr MacIver?'

'Yes.'

'Mr Hammerstein is away for a week.'

Damn, Jason had forgotten that. 'OK. Can I speak to Mr Cohen then, please?'

Another pause.

'Mr MacIver. Mr Cohen has asked me to tell you that having given the matter due consideration he is not able to offer you representation at this time.' She said it mechanically as if it were something she said fifty times a day.

'Hold on a minute. Joy Chivas intro . . .'

'Thank you for your interest.'

The phone went dead, the dialling tone buzzing in his ear. He patiently re-dialled the number.

'Nancy Dockery please.'

'Who's calling?'

'A friend.'

'I must have a name.'

'Eh, George . . .'

'Mr MacIver, Ms Dockery is unable to be of assistance to you either. Goodbye. Please don't call again.'

What on earth was he going to do now? Jason took the card Martha Morris had given him out of his wallet. He dialled the number.

'Hello?'

'Martha?'

'No . . . wait please.' He heard the woman calling Martha to the phone.

'Hello, Martha Morris.' Her voice sounded deep and rich and full of warmth and humour.

'It's Jason . . .'

The warmth and humour disappeared. 'What do you want?'

'I thought we were friends.'

'What gave you that idea?'

'Listen, Hanna and I . . .'

'I know. Hanna told me. You're plain stupid, aren't you? Just stupid. I told you. I gave you good advice.'

'I know, but I . . .'

'Piss off, Jason,' she said and slammed the phone down.

The phone box was hot, its plastic covering concentrating the sun. Jason was sweating. He looked at his watch. It was too early to call Joy Chivas in London.

He phoned directory enquiries and asked for the number of Bill Talbot's house. There were ten W Talbots in Beverly Hills and six in Bel Air and he hadn't the slightest idea of the address. The idea of calling Helen Talbot was probably useless too. Hanna would have got there first.

Looking up and down the Strip Jason could see the big black letters on Hammerstein and Cohen's building at 9000 Sunset. He started walking towards it. He had a feeling that the one person who wouldn't give him the bum's rush was Nancy Dockery. And if she did at least she could do it to his face.

It was a long way. In a car it had taken minutes, but on foot it took forever. The pavement stones were hot and made his feet ache.

Jason was in no mood to think about what had happened. There was no point. He had made a mistake and there was no way back. Hanna had presumably spoken to everyone he had met and, from Martha's reaction, invented some story about him. She'd clearly got to Hammerstein and Cohen too.

Finally he arrived outside 9000 Sunset. He looked at his watch. When did they finish? Six, six-thirty. It was going to be a long wait. Nancy had to have a car, everyone in LA did and she had to park it in the parking lot he had used. As quietly as he could he sneaked up to the garage entrance. The attendant was busy reading *Sports Illustrated*. Ducking his head below the level of the glass booth, Jason edged passed. Finding a spot where he could see the lift doors he hunkered down by one of the cars on the hard concrete floor and waited. At least the garage was cool. He felt the sweat drying on his forehead.

The lift was busy. A constant stream of people arrived and went to their cars. But Jason didn't expect Nancy to leave before six. By six forty-five, however, he was giving up hope. By seven he was convinced she'd either gone home early or was the only person in the whole city who didn't drive to work. At seven-fifteen the lift doors opened and Nancy Dockery walked out with another man, a small, stout man, almost entirely bald, who Jason recognised from the family photo he had seen on his desk as George Hammerstein. So much for him being away for a week.

The couple were walking towards him.

'So we'll sort that out in the morning,' Hammerstein was saying.

'First thing,' Nancy replied.

'Night, then.'

'Night.'

Hammerstein climbed into a white Cadillac Seville and drove off. Nancy walked on to a blue Volkswagen Beetle.

'Hi!' Jason said, coming up behind her.

'Hi there.' Nancy's face broke into an unreserved smile. She seemed genuinely pleased to see him. 'What are you doing here?'

'I need a friend.'

'Sounds bad.'

'It is.'

'Oh dear. Better get in, then. You fancy something to eat?'

She was wearing a tight short black dress, her bust trying to escape from its V-neckline, her legs hardly encumbered by its inch or two of skirt. Today her legs were bare.

'Anything,' he said.

She unlocked the door of the Beetle, put her briefcase on the backseat and lent across to open the passenger door for Jason. The car seemed tiny inside after the cars he had been used to, the Caddys and Mercedes, and Rolls Royces.

'So . . . ?' she asked as she turned out of the garage and on to the Strip.

'George Hammerstein wasn't away.'

'No. He told me to tell you that. He didn't seem very interested in talking to Hanna Silverstein.'

'Obviously not.'

'I'm sorry, but what could I do? I felt really bad about it.'

'I'm not blaming you. Did Hanna call him this afternoon?'

'Yes. I don't know what was said, though. I don't know if it was about you.'

'It was. I called too but got very short shrift. They wouldn't even put me through to you.'

'Really? First I heard . . .'

He told her everything this time. Well, almost everything. There was no point in lying. He left out a few details but none of the basic facts. By the time they reached her small bungalow he had been talking for almost an hour.

'Home,' she announced, pulling into an off-road parking

spot amongst a riot of overgrown shrubs. 'Not much but it's home.'

She led the way past the side of the house into a small back garden which had been planted with so many different flowers and shrubs it was a jungle of colours and greenery. There was a small patio.

'Sit out here. I'll get us a drink.'

Jason sat at a small table. Nancy was back in minutes with a bottle of red wine and two glasses. She poured the wine and Jason drunk eagerly.

'Now use my phone.'

'What?'

'Call Joy Chivas in England.'

'Thanks. I can't pay you back now but I will.'

'I heard George talking to Cohen this afternoon. They must have told our receptionist to give you the brush off.'

'I'd love to know what Hanna told him.'

Nancy showed him the phone. Inside the house was pretty, decorated with flair and imagination. The hall was covered with a collection of antique keys.

He got through to London.

'Joy Chivas, please,' he said.

'Who's calling?'

'Jason MacIver. I'm calling from Los Angeles so could you make it quick.'

There was a loud click. 'Jason?'

'Joy . . .'

'Jason, I have only one thing to say to you. If you choose to behave with such total unprofessionalism I'm afraid I am not prepared to represent you any more. I can't have the reputation of this agency connected with someone like you.'

'What am I supposed to have done?'

'I don't think I want to discuss that . . .'

'I thought you were supposed to be on my side.'

'Goodbye, Jason. And don't call again.'

For the fourth time that day Jason's ear was assailed by a slammed telephone and an abrupt dialling tone.

He wandered out on to the patio. Nancy wasn't there. He went back inside and found her in the kitchen making a salad, in a large white bowl.

'Well?'

'I'm fired.'

'Fired?'

'Unprofessional conduct.'

'What does that mean?'

'Calling Hanna a bitch?'

'From what you've told me she is one.'

'So what am I going to do?'

'Go back to England . . .'

'I've got no ticket. I've got no money. Anyway, if I go back it'll look like everything she's said about me is true.'

'Well, I'm going to cook you a delicious dinner. Then we'll talk about it.'

Against all the odds Jason found he was hungry. She cooked two steaks and baked potatoes and salad. They ate ice cream from her freezer. They finished the first bottle of wine and opened a second. Nancy ate with gusto, enjoying everything, eating everything. As he had noticed over their lunch she was well read and had an opinion on any subject he cared to name. It made a change to be talking about something other than the film business, especially after the events of the day. Not that he could stop himself seething inside. Nor could he imagine what in the world he was going to do.

They took coffee into the living room where two small sofas were neatly arranged around a fake log-fire.

'Are you easily shocked?' Nancy asked.

'After what I've seen in Hollywood . . .'

Nancy had taken two video cassettes from her briefcase.

'I've got this friend who works in a video copying company just down from the office . . . These are the latest, hot from the presses . . .'

'Movies?'

'Sort of . . . I . . . eh . . .'

'Blue movies!'

'I suppose I sort of . . . well, I collect them.'

'Porn?'

'Yah. Hard-core porn. Are you shocked?'

'It turns you on?'

'In a word, yes. Don't know why. I know a lot of my friends think I'm nuts. Women aren't supposed to get turned on by watching. Not like men.'

She slotted one of the videos into the player under the television.

'Nancy, look, you've been really great to me. But hadn't I better find a hotel, or something?'

'You haven't got any money.'

'That's true, but . . .'

'Jason, I think you're an incredibly attractive man. If you don't stay with me tonight I'll be insulted. I'll also develop a severe inferiority complex thinking you'll sleep with Hanna and not me. So just relax. Let's watch the movie then go to bed. Deal?'

'Deal.' It was an offer he couldn't refuse.

Nancy kissed him lightly on the lips as if to seal the bargain, then turned on the television. She sat on the sofa next to him, curled her legs up under her and turned the video on by remote control.

There was a fanfare of music and credits rolled: 'Hollywood Blues Productions present *The Pussy Trap*, starring Camilla Potts.'

'Camilla!' Jason shouted. 'Camilla?'

'Didn't you know? Over here Camilla Potts is the new Linda Lovelace. She's the number one star in porn.'

'My God, I had no idea.' Jason's mind was reeling. He'd fucked a porn queen.

'Sure. She's a big star. The biggest. No wonder – look at her body . . .' Nancy said. And there it was in all its glory on her television screen. Camilla, naked apart from a pair of sheer black stockings and a thin black suspender belt and very high-heeled shoes, her shaven sex looking as though it had been oiled, was leading a rather unattractive man into a sparsely furnished bedroom. There, on a large double bed, was another couple already engaged in intercourse. For the next twenty minutes the four bodies engaged in every combination of sexual activity.

Nancy got up, and switched the tape off in the middle of Camilla attempting to take both cocks in her mouth at the same time.

'Let's try the other one.'

'You collect these?'

'A girl's got to have a hobby,' Nancy replied coyly. She slotted the other tape into the machine. 'You're shocked,' she said, sitting back on the sofa next to him.

'Nothing shocks me any more,' he said, and meant it, still reeling from the discovery of Camilla's profession.

Nancy operated the remote control. Another-fanfare. Another set of credits: 'Hollywood Blues presents *The Velvet Room* starring Camilla Potts.'

This time the screen went dark, almost blank. He heard a voice.

'*No . . . No . . . please.*' It was Camilla's voice.

'*Come out where I can see you,*' another voice said. He recognised that voice vaguely too.

'*No.*'

'*Do it.*'

'*No.*'

The picture came into focus. Jason recognised the dark burgundy drapes that hung in the room at exactly the same time as he realised the second voice on the tape was his. He saw the three-panelled screen and watched as an athletic, muscled blond man strode up to it and brought Camilla out by the wrist.

'*Please don't hurt me,*' she said on the tape.

'*Stand still . . .*' his voice said.

Camilla looked frightened. Of course, it had all been an act. From the angle of the shot he calculated that the camera must have been behind the mirror.

'Jason!' Nancy cried, clutching his knee. His face on the screen had just come into shot. 'It's you . . . It's you . . .'

Jason said nothing. They watched silently as the scene

210

unfolded, every detail caught on tape. That's why she'd changed position when he'd thrown her out of the pool of light. ('*I didn't tell you to move*,' his voice castigated.)

Nancy was spellbound. She watched as Camilla took his cock in her mouth. She watched as his cock thrust into her anus.

'*Oh yes, yes . . .*' Camilla screamed from the television.

Eventually the screen went blank.

'God, Jason . . .' Nancy said. She was looking at him with a strange expression on her face, her mouth slack, her breathing shallow. 'That was so exciting.'

'What am I going to do?'

'About what?'

'No one will ever employ me again.'

'Rubbish. Lots of star actors have started in porn.'

He did not reply. He had a sudden flash of memory, probably brought on by seeing Camilla again. He was in that strange room with Harry and Cynthia and Camilla was staring through the glass. Beside her was a video camera.

'I think there's another one.'

'What?'

'Last night, I told you, when I was drugged. Camilla was there, I think. And a camera.'

'I'll see if I can get a copy. God, Jason . . .'

'What?'

'You're a . . . you're in very good shape.' Nancy's hand had not left the top of his knee.

'If you hadn't got these I might never have found out.'

Nancy's hand worked up his thigh. 'Jason, Jason . . .' she said. 'This may not be a good time for you I know but . . .'

'What?'

'Can't you guess?'

'Guess what?'

'Jason, I've just watched you giving Camilla Potts . . . well . . . I mean isn't it time we went to bed?'

Before she could say any more he kissed her hard on the mouth, pushing her back on the sofa. He could feel her passion, it was oozing out of her body, like sweat. He already had an erection. Watching himself with Camilla had turned him on too. He looked good. He looked strong. At acting school he'd seen himself on video but this was the first time he'd seen himself doing anything for real. Secretly, down deep inside, he was excited. Not only sexually excited but emotionally. Camilla had given him a role to play, however bizarre, and he'd played it. He was convincing, a convincing master. The content didn't matter, he told himself. He'd given his performance and the camera had loved it. He had the evidence in his arms. He could feel Nancy Dockery melting under him.

They broke the kiss.

'I feel so sexy, so turned on,' Nancy said. 'Do you mind?'

'Why should I mind?'

She got up and took the video from the machine. 'There's a video in the bedroom. I want to see it again,' she explained, taking his hand and leading him through the short hall to the bedroom.

The bedroom was larger than the living room and very untidy. A bank of louvred doors along one wall was filled to bursting with clothes. They spilled out in a profusion of colours. A large chest of drawers was equally full, so congested none of the drawers would close properly.

'Sorry about the mess. I keep meaning to throw all this junk out . . .'

The television and video were on the chest of drawers facing the bed. She slotted the tape into the machine. Mounted on the wall nearby was a unit of three shelves, filled with video tapes. Some, like the ones from today, had no titles or covers. Others Jason could see had very explicit photographs and titles, like *Clockwork Banana*, *Blue Weekend*, and *Sex for Six*.

Nancy rewound the tape. 'My collection,' she said.

'So I see.'

Nancy felt physically hot. She squirmed her thighs together almost imperceptibly, her body obeying a rhythm of its own. She still felt breathless, her heart fluttering with nervous excitement.

There was an old fashioned black iron bedstead and the counterpane was a patchwork quilt, adding to the impression of disorder in the room.

Jason sat on the edge of the bed.

The tape clunked as it rewound fully. Automatically the video switched to play mode. Nancy turned off the overhead light. She picked up a red scarf that had fallen from the chest of drawers and draped it over the bedside light. The room was bathed in a rosy glow.

'So now you know all my secrets.' She came and stood in front of him, taking the pins out of her hair so it fell over her shoulders.

'What secrets?'

'My tapes . . .'

'Well, you certainly know mine.'

'I'm so turned on, Jason. Seeing you like that . . .'

From the television the fanfare announced the production credits.

'I'm wet. I can feel it.'

She took hold of the hem of the dress and pulled it over her head. The triangle of her belly was right in front of his eyes. She was wearing a pair of high-cut tanga-style panties in a beige colour. The panties looked as though they had been inflated, puffed up by the thickness of pubic hair beneath the thin cotton. There was so much the panties contained only a fraction. It escaped the cotton V on all sides. There was a thick trail right up to her belly button! It grew in profusion out on either side and right down between her thighs, and at the top of her thighs themselves. It spread out everywhere, like a lawn, untended and untrimmed.

Nancy threw the dress on the floor. Jason looked up as she unhooked her breasts from the matching beige bra which fastened at the front. Her breasts quivered as they were set free, big soft mounds of flesh. They matched Nancy's body perfectly. She was not fat but nor was she skinny. Her limbs were large, her thighs strong and powerful looking, her shoulders square, her arms muscled. She was a big girl in every way.

Deliberately, Nancy pushed her tits into Jason's face.

'*Come out where I can see you*,' Jason heard his voice say on the television. 'You're beautiful,' he said in reality.

'Can I?'

'Can you what?'

'Can I show you . . .'

Before he could reply Nancy kicked her shoes off and pulled down her panties. The hair that had been trapped under them

214

sprung up like little seedlings uncurling in the sun. She combed them, running her fingers through the black curls. Jason saw one finger dip lower.

'I want to see you . . .' she said.

She didn't mean the real him, she meant the screen him. She lay back on the bed, opening her legs and watching as Camilla was tied to the frame. She imagined herself in that position, the leather straps biting into her wrists. With one hand she took her breast and kneaded it aggressively, while the other stroked the furry animal that lived between her thighs. Parting the hair she strummed at her clitoris.

'Do you think I should shave like her?'

'No . . .' he said, his attention torn between Nancy and watching himself on the screen.

'Oh Jason . . .'

Two fingers slipped into her cunt. There was obviously no resistance.

'Did she feel good, Jason? Was she hot?'

'Oh yes,' he said unbuttoning his shirt.

'*Please don't gag me, Master,*' Camilla's voice entreated.

'Please don't gag me, Master,' Nancy repeated, her foot touching Jason's back. Her thumb was working her clitoris now, not gently and subtly but viciously, in a blur of motion, the motion that her body demanded. It was like a fantasy. Night after night she would masturbate watching these videos, her body straining for release, straining to imagine what the cocks she saw on the screen would feel like, be like. Big wet cocks, hard and veiled and gnarled. What would they feel like inside her? Now, tonight, it was coming true. The screen cock was going to be real, come alive just for her. Was that why she felt so excited, so impossibly hot?

She was coming like she had never come before. There was no part of her body or mind that wasn't urging her on, that wasn't strung out, eager for her climax. Expertly her fingers played the tune her body requested. She watched the cock on the screen probe Camilla's bound and helpless body, knowing it would be inside her soon, that same cock, knowing she'd feel it for herself. She watched the eyes on the screen looking at her, then focused on the real eyes watching her as she wanked so wantonly. Then her eyes closed and she surrendered to the massive flood of feeling that arced through her body like electricity. She thrust her hips up off the bed, angling her cunt at Jason, wanting him to see its contractions.

She slumped into a wet damp heap, gasping for breath.

Jason stripped off his trousers. On the screen he was releasing Camilla from the wooden trestle, his face masked now in black leather. Nancy opened her eyes. On screen the camera was dwelling on a close-up of Jason's cock. In front of the screen there was the real thing, like a visual echo.

'Oh Jason . . . please . . .' she held out her arms.

His cock was as hard as stone. He knelt between her legs.

'*What now, Master?*' Camilla's voice came from behind him.

'*Kneel, lick my cock . . .*' his voice replied.

Nancy started to sit up ready to obey, confusing the video with reality.

'No,' Jason said, pushing her back.

He fell on her, everything forgotten but his need to bury himself in her open cunt. His cock sank in until he could feel his balls on her arse. This was not a performance. He didn't care about anything but his own pleasure. Nancy's hand found his nipple. The soreness there, where the nipple clips had left their mark, was delicious. He started thrusting with all his strength. Her other hand was on his arse. He felt the red welts react, another wave of pleasure generated in pain as her hand urged him forward.

'Do it. Give it to me . . .'

Nancy was watching the screen over his shoulder. She watched his piercing blue eyes behind the black mask . . .

Jason pumped into her. He could feel her so well, every nook and cranny of her cunt, or so it seemed. Her cunt was deep and tight, it clung to him, sucked on him, melted over him. He knew he wasn't going to be able to stop himself from coming.

Somewhere in all this excitement a thought had come to him. In the last days he had had more sex, it seemed, than in the whole of the rest of his life, more adventure. He had drowned in sex, in beautiful women, in big breasts and liquid cunts, in feelings and experiences that he would not have believed possible. But most of all he had performed and his performance had been applauded. Women desired him, wanted him; film stars like Martha, producers like Hanna, powerful women like Harry, even little scrubbers like Cynthia. He was good at sex. His body was made for it. He liked it. Look at how Nancy had responded. She'd recognised his power and strength, appreciated his performance, believed it.

Was any of that so bad? He remembered Martha's words – 'Be Hollywood.' Well, if he were honest with himself, if this was Hollywood, the real Hollywood, he loved it. When in Rome . . . That's what he had to do.

'*Bugger me, bugger me* . . .' Camilla's voice was screaming.

'Give me your spunk . . .' Nancy screamed no less emphatically.

His cock jerked violently. His eyes rolled back in his head, the nerves at the back of his eyeballs giving him an exquisite sensation. His body locked completely, all movement stopped but the spasms of his cock as it flung his spunk into the depths of Nancy Dockery's willing body.

Eventually, after what seemed to be a long, long time, his cock softened and was expelled by the pressure of Nancy's cunt – a moment that made her gasp with an aftershock of pleasure. He rolled off her.

'You're a star,' she said, as though reading his mind.

'I was being selfish.'

'I don't mean the sex. I mean the video. That's going to be a big hit. Take it from an expert. She's good. She always has been. But the guys are usually wet. Big cocks and wimpy looking. No class. You've got the cock and class.'

'Thank you,' he said. He knew it was true.

'Of course, there's one thing that remains to be seen.'

Nancy got up off the bed. The thick pubic hair was even more matted now, plastered down to her body by the wetness they had created. She went over to the chest of drawers and turned off the video and television. From one drawer she pulled out four long scarves. From another she took a pair of stockings, in a shimmery flesh colour, and a white suspender belt. Sitting in a chair opposite the bed she rolled the stockings up her long powerful legs. Jason could see the lips of her sex through the wet hair.

'And what's that,' he asked.

She stood up when both stockings were in place, and clipped

the suspender belt around her waist. It was lacy, a wide band of white lace, its suspenders ruched in white satin. She pulled the welt of the stocking into the loops of the suspenders, pushing the little rubber ring through the metal hoop. The stockings were stretched taut over her broad thighs, the flesh above the nylon, by contrast, seeming almost obscenely exposed and open. The tops of the stockings, the satin suspenders and the suspender belt itself, framed the abundant, sprawling growth of hair that spread out from the apex of her thighs.

'Your recovery time,' she said.

She smoothed each of her legs in turn, using her hands to make sure the stockings were completely even. He watched her big breasts hanging down from her chest as she stooped, great mounds of pendulant flesh. When she stood up straight again she parted her legs slightly and put her hands on her hips, arms akimbo. She looked like an Amazon warrior, the blaze of excitement in her eyes undiminished.

'How do I compare with Camilla?' she asked.

'You're beautiful,' he said.

'Then the only question is how long it takes you to get another erection . . . It didn't take you long on the tape.'

Nancy tied one of the long scarves firmly to the corner post at the foot of the bedstead. She repeated the process with the other three scarves at the other three corners.

'And there was something else on the tape I would like to try . . .'

# Chapter Eleven

'Jason?'

'Yes.' he recognised the voice but couldn't put a name to it.

'It's Camilla.'

'Camilla! How did you find me?' He was sitting in Nancy Dockery's kitchen, wearing her bathrobe and drinking her coffee. Nancy had gone to work an hour before.

'I called Hammerstein and Cohen. Nancy told me.'

'That was clever. You heard what happened, then?' Jason was not sure whether he should be angry with Camilla or not. While he tried to make his mind up his voice remained cool.

'I've got to see you. It's urgent. I've got some good news.'

'Another hidden camera.'

'You've seen it?'

'Yes.'

'That saves me explaining then.'

'Explaining what?'

'Listen, Jason, don't be pissed off. That tape could be the best thing that ever happened to either of us. Len Furey. You know Len Furey. The director. He's a friend of mine. Friend friend not bed friend. Well, he's really impressed with you. He's got a part . . . wants to meet you.'

'Len Furey. *The* Len Furey.'

'Sure.'

Any anger he felt with Camilla evaporated instantly.

'Len Furey wants to meet me because he saw me in that porn tape with you?'

'You got it.'

'When?'

'Now. I'll come by and pick you up. There's a part for me too, apparently. A straight part. Can you be ready in half-an-hour?'

'What about Hanna?'

'What about her?'

'I thought you two were friends.'

'We are.'

'So? Hasn't she warned you off, told you terrible things about me? She has everyone else.'

'Hanna behaves like a petulant child sometimes, Jason. If she can't have something she doesn't want anyone to have it.'

'And if she calls Len Furey and warns him off?'

'Len won't give a shit. And if you get the part and it's a success she'll be begging you to work with her like nothing ever happened. That's Hollywood.'

The Culver City Studios were more or less identical to Burbank. A little smaller, perhaps, but otherwise the same huge buildings and the same back lots filled with the left-over sets from a hundred different films that it was cheaper to leave standing than knock down. Another New York street, like the one at the wrap party, dominated most of the space.

By twelve-thirty Camilla was parking her extensively restored MGB soft-top outside the offices in the administration block. As always, she looked stunning. Today she looked as though she had just breezed up from the beach, a floral print bikini covered by a long split skirt in the same material, the bra struggling to contain the bounty of her breasts, the strip of flesh between the bottom of the bra and the top of the skirt, a reminder of the complexion of her nakedness.

By one o'clock they were sitting in the studio commissary eating the ubiquitous salad and sipping Evian. Len Furey didn't drink, which was a considerable plus as far as Jason was concerned. A blue-bound script lay on the table in front of them and Len had explained that he needed an actor with a real sexual charisma.

'We've got to believe that any woman would really fall for this guy. Otherwise the whole film falls to pieces. You get it?'

'I think so.'

'And from what I've seen on the tape . . .'

Jason thought he felt himself blushing. He hoped it didn't show.

Len Furey looked like an academic. He was slim and white-haired, his hair wiry and thick. His face was attractive, rather elongated, with a long nose, and a dark five o'clock shadow that looked as though he had to shave twice a day. He wore corduroy trousers, a plaid shirt and a grey cardigan with a rolled collar.

'So what happens now?' Jason asked

'Go home, read the script and call me.'

By three o'clock Jason was sitting in Nancy Dockery's front room reading the last three pages of the script. It was wonderful, the part, his part, even better. He threw it down on the sofa as he finished the last page and leapt into the air. This was it. His big break. He'd known it would come. He thought it had with Hanna Silverstein but that had been a false dawn. This was different.

He knew with total certainty that this part in this film could make him a star.

They drove up into the Hollywood Hills to a restaurant that had panoramic views over the Los Angeles basin. Seated at a table by the window they could even see the lights on the oil rigs out at sea.

Nancy had insisted on buying Jason a suit. She insisted they had champagne and that she was paying the bill. He could take her out as soon as he got his first cheque.

The restaurant was smart, white linen and sparkling glass, tables laid with little bunches of white flowers, waiters in tailcoats, the space between the diners enough to make it impossible to overhear conversations. Not surprisingly since, according to Nancy, it was filled with executives from rival studios. There were also the usual sprinkling of television and film stars, some with their wives and some with their lovers, and some having earnest conversations with their agents.

'A star is born,' Nancy said, raising her champagne glass.

'Thanks to you.'

'Why me?'

'I'd have been sleeping on the beach without you.'

'Don't worry, I'll make you pay . . .' she laughed.

Even among the glitterati in the room Nancy looked impressive. She had piled her hair high on her head revealing her long sinewy neck. The plunging neckline of the navy blue dress revealed a dark shadow of cleavage, and its skirt, as was her style, hid no more than an inch or two of her full strong thighs, encased in shimmering silvery nylon.

Nancy was the sort of woman who made men stare, long and hard and lustfully. They did not stare for objective reasons because they admired her beauty like some fine painting. She was not that sort of woman. They stared simply because they wanted to fuck her.

'I'd better move to a hotel.'

'Why?'

'I can't go on staying with you . . .'

'Why not? I realise after Hanna's it's not . . .'

'I didn't mean that. I just thought you'd . . .'

'Jason. Don't think. Stay with me. No ties. No emotions. Stay until you get settled. Unless you'd rather not?'

'I was hoping you'd say that,' he grinned.

Over dinner of Oysters Rockefeller, Maine lobsters and white chocolate mousse Jason described the plot of the film.

'And Camilla?'

'Camilla?'

'She's in it too?'

'Apparently, there's a part that's very right for her.'

'Do you like her?'

'I hardly know her.'

'It's not that I'm jealous, or anything. Quite the reverse.'

'What's the reverse of not being jealous?'

'I'm . . . I'm very attracted to her, if I'm honest with myself.'

'Really?'

'I've seen all her videos. There's something about her that turns me on. I don't think I'm lesbian . . . it's just something about her. We'd better stop talking about this . . .'

'I'll invite her round.'

'Don't joke.'

'I'm not joking.'

'Maybe it's better kept as a fantasy.'

'You're bound to meet her anyway.'

'I suppose so.'

They drank espresso coffee and ate the petit fours that came on a rectangular silver salver.

'There's something else I have to ask Camilla,' Jason said.

'What's that?'

*The Velvet Room.* That's what they called it, wasn't it?'

'Yes.'

'Well, it was made in Hanna's summerhouse. I thought it was there for her own amusement. Apparently not. Martha Morris told me she was into porn, remember?'

'Yes.'

'Well, it must be true. That two-way mirror, a camera crew . . .'

'True. You better ask her. It might be useful.'

'She has to know something about it at least.'

The conversation turned to other things and on the drive home they said little. Jason stroked Nancy's neck and watched her as she drove, feeling a warm lump of contentment in the pit of his stomach that was only partially to do with his career. He was a very lucky boy all round.

Nancy unlocked the front door and walked straight through into the bedroom, leaving Jason to lock up.

'Zip,' she indicated as soon as he joined her again.

The zip sang as it parted. She stepped out of the dress and pulled off the tights. She had worn no panties.

'I wondered why that waiter nearly choked when you dropped your napkin and he picked it up.'

'I'm feeling wanton. It's something about you. You make me feel turned on all the time I'm with you. Even when I'm not. It was hard to concentrate on work today.'

She came into his arms and whispered in his ear. 'And I've been getting ideas . . .'

'What ideas?'

'Take your clothes off.'

He slipped out of his jacket and shirt. Nancy opened one of the drawers in the chest under the television and took something from a long paper wrapping. She hid it behind her back. Jason slipped off his shoes and socks. Nancy's nakedness, the marvellous voluptuousness of her body, had already given him an erection. He undid his trousers and pulled them off with his underpants.

'Well . . .' she said, circling his cock with one hand. 'So hard already?'

'What have you got there?'

'I went shopping. It was difficult to choose but in the end . . .' She brought the riding crop out from behind her back. 'I chose this one. Will you do it to me, Jason? What you did to Camilla on the tape?'

'Is that what you want?' He took the crop from her hand and swung it through the air testing its weight and flexibility.

Nancy's body flinched involuntarily. 'Oh yes, will you . . . Master.'

'I am your Master,' he said, trying to remember the dialogue from the tape.

'Yes, you are. Please, Master . . .'

'Bend over the bed.'

She obeyed immediately, her plump heavy buttocks pointing up at him, their deep cleft fringed with her abundant pubic hair. He raised the crop without a word. He could see her body quivering in anticipation.

'Oh yes . . . yes . . .' she moaned.

The crop whistled through the air and smacked down across the meatiest part of her rump. A red welt appeared instantly. He aimed a second stroke. A second welt. She gasped at each stroke, a sound redolent of pure pleasure. He could see the compressed lips of her sex beginning to moisten.

'Kneel up on the bed,' he ordered, using his dominant tone.

'Yes, Master.' She rested her head on the sheets, her knees on her chest, her bum in the air.

The crop whistled again. She knew she would come on the next stroke. She pressed the top of her thighs into her sex. Her clitoris was throbbing and wet. Her mind was on fire as much as her arse. She'd seen him do this on the tape, seen it done on other tapes, but never experienced it before. Never dared to ask another lover. But with Jason anything was possible.

As the crop slashed across her meaty rump her body exploded, out of control, pitching her forward flat on the bed as her nerves screamed out with pleasure.

Jason threw the whip aside, scrambled up on to the bed, pulled her legs apart and thrust between them, his navel rubbing her tortured arse. She screamed as he entered her, a scream of undiluted passion, uninhibited, the noise of an animal. She was an animal, but an animal that knew what it wanted next.

'Jason, Jason . . . please, bugger me. Bugger me, Jason . . .'

The words made her come again. It was not the last time she came that night.

'You're not going to like this, Jason.'

'Like what?' he said, feeling his heart sinking already.

It was one week later and he was sitting in Len Furey's office in the Culver City Studios with Camilla.

'I've lost half the money for the film,' Furey said.

'Lost?'

'Half the finance has pulled out.'

'What does that mean?' Jason tried to stay calm.

'It means everything's on hold till I come up with another two point five million . . .'

Jason noticed Len Furey's fingers. They were incredibly long and slender. He was pressing them together in an attitude of prayer, his elbows on his desk. Jason felt curiously like laughing. For a week he had had the world in his pocket. He had been walking on air. He should have known it was too good to be true. Nothing in life was that easy, especially nothing in Hollywood.

'However,' Furey said.

'Is this the good news?' Camilla asked. She was disappointed too. Her part was not as big as Jason's but it was a good part. It required her to do more than take off her clothes. She wanted desperately to get into 'straight' roles. Her body was her fortune but it wouldn't last forever.

'Except the good news you'll probably think of as bad.'

'Very cryptic,' Jason said.

Furey threw a black-bound script over the desk to Jason.

The cut-out window in its cover revealed the title: *Escape of the Whores*.

'They want me to direct this.'

'Porn?' Jason asked, knowing the answer. He had flicked open the title page. Hollywood Blues Production was stamped under the title.

'There's a part for you. It'll take four weeks. I should be able to find the rest of the money in that time. At least you'll earn some money.'

'I've already turned this down,' Camilla said.

'But that was before I was involved, right? Let's all do it together.'

'You're prepared to direct porn?' Jason said. Len Furey had always been an idol. He had directed two of the best films Jason had ever seen.

'You want the truth, Jason?'

'Yes.'

'I've directed a lot of stuff for Hollywood Blues. I've been broke more times than I care to mention. Ex-wives. And I used to booze. I had to earn money. Everyone does it in Hollywood. It's good money.'

'I've got to earn money too.' Jason couldn't go on living off Nancy Dockery.

'They'll pay over the odds if you do it together. After *The Velvet Room* they're keen to get you two together again . . .'

'And if I don't agree?'

Len Furey smiled indulgently. 'Everyone gets one break, Jason. Some people take it, some people don't. My film will be your break. But if you're not around by the time I get the money . . .'

They had driven straight back to Nancy's house and sat in her living room sharing a bottle of red wine.

'It's easy,' Camilla said. 'You did it before.'

'I know. But last time I didn't know there was a camera there, did I?' Jason said pointedly.

'You think that'll make a difference?'

'I don't know. This is going to be on film. There'll be a big crew . . .'

'So we'll get Len to give you a test.'

'A screen test?' Jason laughed.

'What's so funny?'

'That's why I came here, remember. For Hanna's screen test.'

'You'll be all right. There's nothing to it.'

'Talking of Hanna . . .'

'Yes.'

'*The Velvet Room* . . .'

'Yes?'

'Tell me about it.'

'Tell you what?'

'Whose idea was it? Hanna's?'

'I can't tell you, Jason.'

'I mean, there's that two-way mirror. All that equipment . . .'

'Hanna used to be into . . . well, she liked to film herself . . . in certain situations. That's why she had that room built. It sort of expanded from there. Let's leave it at that. I shouldn't have told you that much.'

'And Harriet Teitelbaum?'

'The answer's yes.'

'Yes what?'

'I was there. You were too far gone by that time.'

'And they filmed it?'

'Yes, but not for release. Harry keeps a private collection. She likes me to be on some of them. She pays well over the odds . . .'

'And there were people watching?'

'It's like a little theatre. She invites her friends.'

'My God . . . This is some town.'

'Hi.' Nancy Dockery, the key to her front door still in her hand, walked into the room. Her other hand was clutching a brown paper bag of groceries. Jason saw her eyes light on Camilla.

'Camilla Potts . . . Nancy Dockery.' Jason said.

Nancy put down the shopping and shook Camilla's hand. She was blushing slightly in her excitement.

'You're more beautiful in the flesh,' Nancy said, and meant it. Camilla was wearing a leopard-skin print leotard and matching leggings. The leotard had a high neck but was sleeveless.

'You've seen my films?'

'I'm ashamed to admit I've seen all of them.'

'Really? That's unusual.'

'You are very beautiful.'

'Thank you. Listen, I better go . . .'

'Stay. I mean, why don't you stay for dinner? There's plenty.'

'That would be nice . . .'

Camilla's eyes were looking at Nancy, admiring the lines of her body, the large curve of her breasts, the meaty contours of her thighs. Nancy was wearing a suit, its jacket tailored into her waist, its skirt a little longer than her usual length but tight around her arse. Under the jacket her blouse revealed no cleavage.

'You'd better tell her the bad news,' Camilla said.

'What bad news?'

Jason told her. 'And if you say "That's Hollywood", I'm leaving.'

'Well, at least it's not completely folded.' Nancy said. 'And . . .'

'I know what you're going to say.'

'Of course, you two together again in . . .' Nancy suddenly stopped herself, realising what she was saying. She blushed in earnest this time, her face a deep red. 'I'll get the dinner . . .'

They ate outside in the balmy evening air. Nancy grilled some big Pacific prawns and made a big salad and a dish of spicy rice. They consumed a whole deep-dish American apple pie and drank three bottles of red wine between them. Nancy and Camilla talked of people they knew in the business, exchanging gossip and rumours, mostly on matters sexual. In Hollywood everyone seemed to know everything about everyone's sexual preferences and partners. He could have added a few of his own revelations but kept quiet.

The wine and the air and the endless chattering of the cicadas was wonderfully relaxing. Assuming he could manage to perform in front of a film crew what did it really matter if he did *Escape of the Whores*? It could even be fun, he thought. It could even be exciting, it might even be sexy. And if, at the end of it, Len Furey got the money for his film, then that would be the pot of gold at the end of the rainbow. The depression Jason had felt in Len Furey's office was lifting. Sitting alone with two beautiful women might have something to do with it, of course.

He looked from Nancy to Camilla. Though they were both brunettes they were completely different in their attractiveness. Camilla was definitely the more beautiful of the two in purely visual terms; Nancy exuded an animal attraction. What made Camilla so popular in porn was that she looked so classy and refined but could behave with such sexual abandon. Looking at Nancy, on the other hand, the sexual agenda was clear, sex seemed to ooze from every pore of her big strong body. It was a fascinating combination.

The physical differences made it more so. Camilla's eyes were the lightest of browns, Nancy's dark deep brown. Camilla's hair was short, Nancy's so long that when she let it down she could practically sit on it. Their breasts were both full and heavy, though Camilla's were more rounded and higher, but between their legs the bare, carefully shaven sex of Camilla was in sharp contrast to the chaos of hair that lay between and over and under Nancy's legs.

In the week he had lived with Nancy he had got to know her well enough to sense her excitement. There was a growing rapport between the two women. Jason knew what was in Nancy's mind.

Nancy got up to make coffee, leaving Camilla and Jason alone.

'She's great.'

'I know. I've been very lucky.'

Camilla gazed into the colourful shrubbery. Her forefinger stroked her lower lip.

When Nancy brought the coffee back she was smiling. She poured and distributed the coffee without sitting down.

'I almost forgot,' she said. 'I drove over to Rodeo Drive

at lunchtime. I brought you a surprise.'

'What sort of surprise?' Jason asked. He could see Nancy's eyes were full of mischief and expectation. She reached behind her head and pulled the pins out of her hair. It cascaded down over her shoulders as she tossed her head to shake it out. She had already discarded the jacket of the suit. Now she started to unbutton the white blouse she wore underneath.

'Do you want me to go?' Camilla said quietly.

The blouse was unbuttoned. Nancy stood in front of Camilla looking straight into her eyes. 'You know I don't.' She unzipped her skirt and let it fall to the stone patio floor. At the same time she stripped off the blouse. The surprise had been meant for Jason. Now it had a wider audience.

'Well?' she asked them both, stepping out of the skirt.

She had gone to the most expensive lingerie shop on Rodeo. She had spent an hour trying on different things but the white satin and lace basque had been the best. It held her big breasts firmly, forcing them into a dark tunnel of cleavage. It cinched her waist, emphasised the flare of her strong hips. The suspenders pulled white stockings, sheer shimmery stockings, taut on her powerful-looking thighs. A pair of matching panties, a tiny triangle of silky white, covered little of the abundance of pubic hair. Against the white, her black curls seemed even thicker and more profuse.

It was up to Camilla. She could have got up and gone home. If she was going she had to go now. She didn't. She got up, all right, but instead of leaving she gazed steadily into Nancy's eyes. Slowly she put her hand out and touched the arch of Nancy's breast above the bra of the basque, letting her hand smooth the soft flesh.

'You're very beautiful,' she said.

'I'd like us to . . . I've seen you so many times . . . I . . .'

'Sh . . .' Camilla said, putting her finger to Nancy's lips. 'I know.'

A light breeze ruffled the luxuriant foliage of Nancy's garden. For a moment there was a sense of infinite possibilities. Both women sat down again. Camilla sipped at her coffee, Nancy finished her wine. Jason remained quiet too. There was nothing to be said. There was nothing that needed to be said.

Eventually Camilla got to her feet. She stroked Nancy's cheek with the back of her hand, then disappeared into the house.

'I bought this for you,' Nancy said. 'I didn't know she'd be here.'

'You look ravishing.'

'I'm very excited.'

'Are you?'

'I've never done it before. I've watched it so many times. Wondered what it would be like.' She lent forward and put her hand on Jason's thigh, squeezing it tightly. Her touch felt electric as though her body was charged up. 'Pity we don't have a video camera . . .'

'Don't remind me.'

'You're going to do it, aren't you? Furey's film.'

'I haven't decided yet.'

Nancy stood up. Jason looked at the magnificent body in the tight corset. It emphasised her big tits and the flare of her hips. At the back her plump arse was almost completely exposed, the panties no more than a white thong between the cleft of her cheeks.

Hand in hand they walked into the bedroom.

Camilla lay naked on the bed. Her legs were open, wide open, and she held both her tits in her hands.

'I've never done this before,' Nancy said, staring at her body. The lack of hair on her sex revealed every detail, every line and crevice.

'Do you want to do it with me?' Camilla asked seriously.

'I didn't know I could feel this way about a woman.' Nancy was seized by an involuntary shudder. Was it nerves or anticipation?

Camilla patted the bed and Nancy dutifully sat where she indicated. Immediately Camilla pulled her down on to the sheets beside her. She pressed her body into the white satin and felt the softness of Nancy's flesh underneath. The pillows of their breasts were forced together, ballooning outwards. Nancy felt her heart beating faster and faster. She kissed Camilla on the mouth or did Camilla kiss her? In her mind's eye she saw *Camilla being kissed by other women, other men on the videos.* Now it was real. The video came to life again, real flesh and blood. Her hesitancy disappeared. She kissed Camilla's neck, her throat, then cupped each of her breasts in turn, to feed them into her mouth. She used her teeth to tease at the nipples, the way she liked men to do it to her. She heard Camilla moan. Her free had moved over Camilla's naked belly and down over the perfectly smooth curve of her pubic bone. Camilla's sex was wet. For the first time in her life she ran her forefinger between the lips of a woman's sex and touched a clitoris. It felt hot, much hotter than she'd expected. Using the same principle - remembering what she liked men to do to her - she stroked the tiny knot of nerves. Camilla moaned again.

Nancy kissed her navel, sliding down the bed so she could kiss Camilla's thighs. She kissed and sucked and licked down to the knees, then came up again, until her mouth was inches, less than inches, away from Camilla's labia. She could smell her perfume - Chanel 19, she thought - mingling with the musky aroma of her sex. She did not hesitate. She drove her mouth forward, carried by her passion now, feeling the soft lips giving way to her tongue, allowing her access to the melting pot beneath. She explored with her tongue, pushing it into Camilla's sex as far as it would go, then circling the entrance as she loved men to do with her. She was not tentative. She knew what she wanted and she was going to get it. She wanted Camilla to come in her mouth, over her tongue. She'd watched her come so many times on tape, now she wanted the reality.

Camilla's hand was pulling at her body. At first she didn't realise why. Then she knew what she wanted. She knelt up, without taking her mouth from Camilla's cunt, and swung her legs over her face so her cunt was poised above Camilla's face.

Camilla hooked her arms around Nancy's meaty, stockinged thighs. With one hand she pulled the thin silk of the panties aside. She levered her head off the bed and anchored her mouth on Nancy's hairy animal of a sex.

Nancy gasped. The two were intricately joined. There was no thought now, only feeling, each mouth working for the other's pleasure. They felt so much. Their breasts pressed between their bodies, nipples as hard as pebbles; their fingers exploring the caverns of their cunts; their tongues licking from anus to clitoris. Nancy's finger slipped into the tightness of Camilla's anus. Camilla immediately did the same. Camilla's tongue tapped out a tattoo on Nancy's clitoris, and Nancy did the same. Everything was matched, echoed, repeated: a chorus of perfect harmony.

Jason slipped out of his clothes, his erection sticking out horizontally in front of him. He could see they were coming now. Their bodies were one, one rhythm, the harmony driving them higher, locking them together until neither woman could distinguish self any more, not tell where one woman began and the other ended. They were so close, so enraptured by sensation it felt as though their pleasure was doubled, though two had become one.

'Oh, oh, oh . . .' Nancy's hot breath exploded against Camilla's sex as she, in turn, felt Camilla's body come, quivering and trembling out of control. Nancy's orgasm drove Camilla deeper, higher. Camilla's had the same effect on Nancy. It went on and on and on, like a rubber ball bouncing off one wall on to another. Finally they surrendered to the impossibility of more. They slumped back on to the bed, a tangled mess of limbs.

Nancy started to giggle. It was infectious. Camilla started to laugh too.

'Why are we laughing?' Camilla asked.

'I never thought it would be so good and . . .'

'And?'

'Jason looks like a man who's lost a dollar and found a cent.'

It was true. Camilla looked at the expression on his face. He wasn't at all sure whether he was surplus to requirements.

'Well, we'd better cheer him up, hadn't we?' Getting up off the bed Camilla knelt in front of him and casually closed her mouth around his cock.

'Did you enjoy the show?' Nancy asked, pulling the tiny, and now sodden, panties down her legs.

'Oh . . .' was all Jason could reply as Camilla's mouth sucked his rock-hard cock.

'I want you to fuck me, Jason.' Nancy said. She turned on to her stomach and thrust her big fleshy arse into the air. 'Like this.'

Camilla released his cock, but holding it in her hand, led him over to the bed by it, like a dog on a lead.

'Guess this is your lucky day,' she said. She kissed him softly. Her mouth tasted of Nancy.

He knelt on the bed. A drop of fluid wept from his cock. He could feel his heart beating rapidly. Slowly he stroked Nancy's thighs, moving his hand from the softness of her skin to the harshness of the nylon.

'Beautiful, isn't she?'

Camilla knelt on the bed behind him, pressing her naked breasts into his shoulders, her hand still circling his cock. As he edged forward she guided it between the lips of Nancy's sex. They were soaking wet. With her hips Camilla bucked forward, pushing her flat navel into Jason's arse, urging him forward in turn. He needed little encouragement. His cock sunk into the depths of Nancy's hot cunt.

He pumped to and fro, feeling Camilla behind him and Nancy in front, a sandwich of soft melting female flesh. He could feel Camilla's cunt radiating heat against his arse, but most of all he could feel her wickedly expert hand between their legs. It wanked at Nancy's clitoris, it circled the shaft of his cock, it cupped and toyed with his balls. Alternating between the two of them it was driving them both wild.

'Give it to her,' she hissed into his ear, leaving her tongue there to trace the whorls, then pushing it deep, right down into the tight sensitive orifice. 'Give it to her . . .' she repeated as she felt Jason's reaction to the intrusion of her tongue.

Nancy was out of control. Her second orgasm flooded through her body, breaking over Camilla's artful finger and Jason's hard cock buried deep inside her. But there was no respite. Camilla did not stop and nor did Jason. Camilla's other hand reached around to her breasts. They had fallen out of the bra of the basque and were swinging in time to Jason's thrusts. Camilla's fingers searched for her nipples. Finding them hard and erect she pinched them both in turn, squeezing the great mounds of flesh back into Nancy's chest. That was enough to send her over the edge again, plunging down into darkness, down into another orgasm, another shattering explosion of feeling raking through every nerve in her body.

Jason felt her cunt contracting around his cock, like a pump sucking in air, sucking and clinging to his rock-hard erection. With this provocation he could not hope to last. Camilla's hands seemed to be everywhere, coaxing, caressing, nipping, wanking. They pinched his nipples too, pinched them hard, made him remember the nipple clips that had been chained there. She pulled his balls and stroked his thighs. He felt her big breasts pressed into his shoulder blades and her navel pumping against his arse as if she was fucking him. He looked down at Nancy's back, the long curve of her spine bisected by the white basque, and the fat plump arse rising to meet his thrusts. He saw his cock, wet and glistening with her juices, on the outward stroke, framed by her thick engorged labia. It looked angry, swollen and red as it plunged back again into the centre of her forest of black curls until he could feel them again on his navel.

He knew he could not last. Two women, two beautiful big-breasted women. The meat in their sandwich. He pushed forward one last time and stopped. There in the heart of Nancy's sex he found the place he was searching for, hot, spongy, silky wet. The perfect place. He felt himself tense. He felt her body clinging to him, her cunt sucking his shaft as if it were a mouth. His eyes rolled back and in the blackness, in his mind's eye, he saw his cock inside her, saw it jerk and spasm, saw the slit of his urethra open and spit out great gobs of white, white spunk, out into the space he had found, then hit the black walls of her cunt. Then he could see nothing. He could only feel. He felt the blackness engulf him in a blanket of pure sexual bliss.

The three collapsed on to the bed, panting for breath, their pulses racing. When Jason opened his eyes, Camilla was kissing Nancy's face, little pecking kisses, over her forehead and cheeks, even over her eyes.

'So nice . . .' Nancy moaned.

They kissed more seriously, mouth on mouth, their bodies pressed together, their legs intertwined, Nancy's thigh hard up against Camilla's shaven sex. Jason could see their tongues vying for position.

Eventually Nancy broke away. She stood up, unhooked the basque, and unclipped the stockings from their suspenders. She sat back on the bed to pull the stockings off her legs.

'It's all right,' she said.

'What's all right?' Camilla asked. Very, very gently she was playing with her sex, running the tip of one finger between her labia, stroking the pink inner moistness, teasing herself by letting it just graze the foothills of her clitoris. Back and forth like a paintbrush.

'I tested it.'

'Tested what?' She brought the tip of her finger to her mouth and sucked it. Her fingernails were bright red. Satisfied she had vacuumed off the trail of juices she returned it to her sex.

'His recovery time.' Camilla and Jason were lying side by side, their heads on the pillow. Nancy inserted her legs between them, her head at the opposite end of the bed. The furry animal of her sex nestled comfortably between her thighs.

'I know. Don't you remember *The Velvet Room*? After he'd buggered me?'

'Oh yes . . . How long did that take?'

'Not more than ten minutes, but there are two of us. We should be able to cut that time down, shouldn't we?'

Nancy, seeing what Camilla was doing to herself, opened her legs too and bent her knees, one foot between Jason's thighs, one between Camilla's. She ran the tip of her finger into her labia, aping exactly what Camilla was doing.

'I'm sure we can. Oh Camilla, you look so sexy.'

'So do you.'

What had started as a gentle exercise, a lazy aimless pleasantry turned quite suddenly into need. The two women's eyes were locked on each other's sex, on each other's manipulation. They watched their fingers stop the long patient strokes, and centre on the tiniest of movements, circling and prodding and probing their clitorises.

Nancy had lain on this bed so many times, wanking herself, watching images on the videos, more to the point, watching this woman, Camilla, as exposed and naked as she was now in reality. She saw Camilla's eyes close and knew she was coming a second before her eyes were closed by the flood of feeling her finger and the overwrought images in her mind forced out of her.

'I'm feeling neglected,' Camilla said. They came down slowly, their bodies still full of trills and eddies of residual pleasure.

'We can't have that,' Nancy agreed.

'I need to be fucked.'

'Absolutely. Well, we better get to work on him then, hadn't we? No rest for the wicked.'

'My sentiments exactly,' Camilla said.

Nancy's mouth kissed his ankle, Camilla's his neck. Nancy worked up, kissing and licking and sucking; Camilla worked down. They both had the same goal.

Jason was getting used to people talking about him as if he wasn't there. But this time he didn't mind at all . . .

'Bring him over here.' The voice was hard and cold. She sat in a wing chair in the expensive bedroom.

They had tied his hands behind his back. The other two women dragged him in. They were both big and strong, their fingers digging painfully into his arms. They were both blonde, their muscled bodies naked, their breasts trembling from their exertions. In front of the wing chair they threw him on to the floor.

'Hold him down,' their leader ordered. They obeyed at once, dropping to their knees, their thighs bulging. One held him by the neck until he thought he wasn't going to be able to breathe, the other held his feet.

The leader stood over him. Her body was finer, slim and contoured, her breasts tilted upward, her navel flat. She wore grey cotton knickers, and held a long kitchen knife in her hand. He recognised it. It was from his kitchen.

He flinched as she brought the knife down to his chest and inserted its blade in the front of his shirt at his waist.

'Quite a bonus,' she said. 'We thought the house was empty.' She pulled the knife up towards his chin, ripping his shirt in two.

'Oh yes, quite a bonus. Look at those muscles. You're a big boy, aren't you?'

The knife was back at his waist. It sliced through his belt and down one leg of his trousers. Then back to his waist again to cut the other leg away. She used the tip of the knife to flick away the flap of material that covered his navel. She quickly cut through the side of his underpants and flicked them away too.

'Now . . . look at that girls. He is a big boy.'

They stared down at the man's rampant erection.

'What do you want from me?'

'Speak when you're spoken to, punk,' the woman who held his throat said. The riding crop she held in her other hand slashed down on his chest.

'Oh, the man deserves to know, sisters,' the leader said. 'We want your house. This pretty house. We need somewhere to hole up in for a few days . . .'

The woman put the blade of the knife into the side of her grey knickers and cut them away. They fell to the floor. The man looked up her long slim legs to her sex. It was completely hairless. She was stroking it, like it was an animal.

'We've really lucked out,' the woman at his feet said, her hand snaking up to his cock. 'None of us have had sex for three years.' The hand circled his erection squeezing it impossibly hard. He moaned.

'That's right,' the leader said.

Still standing, she straddled his body, her sex over his cock. Slowly, very slowly she lowered herself until she was squatting, her labia inches from his throbbing glans.

'Cut. That's a print,' Len Furey called. 'And that's a wrap for today, everybody. Seven sharp tomorrow.'

Camilla got to her feet again. An assistant rolled Jason over and untied his hands. The three women were helped into robes and went off to the dressing room. Jason got to his feet as soon as he was freed.

'Great, Jason,' Furey said, as Jason too pulled on a robe. 'You're doing just great.'

'Thanks.' Jason knew it was true. He even had to admit, grudgingly perhaps, that he was enjoying himself.

'Oh, by the way, there's a visitor wants to see you.'

'A visitor?'

'Yah, over in that office.' Furey indicated a door on the far side of the sound stage.

'Who is it?'

Furey came right up to him so none of the rest of the crew would hear. 'She's the woman who puts up the money for this shit. So go and say hello to her and be nice . . . And keep your mouth shut about it. Got it?'

'I don't . . .'

Furey looked at him intensely. 'Buttoned lip. Got it?'

'Got it?'

246

'Be co-operative . . .'

'Do I have to?'

'Jason, this is Hollywood. We're all doing things we don't want to do, kid . . .'

Jason trudged reluctantly over to the office door. He knocked and let himself in. The office was comfortable, well furnished with thick carpet. The windows looked out on to the back lot but the blinds had been drawn and it took a moment for his eyes to adjust after the harsh lighting on the studio floor. A woman in a white dress was lying on a large sofa.

'Hell, Jason, I thought it was time we kissed and made up.'

Hanna Silverstein started unbuttoning the front of her dress . . .

# Lust and Lady Saxon

## L E S L E Y   A S Q U I T H

Pretty Diana Saxon is devoted to her student
husband, Harry, and she'd do anything to make
their impoverished life in Oxford a little easier.
Her sumptuously curved figure and shameless
nature make her an ideal nude model for the
local camera club – where she soon learns
there's more than one way to make a bit on the
side . . .

Elegant Lady Saxon is the most sought-after
diplomat's wife in Rome and Bangkok. Success
has followed Harry since his student days – not
least because of the very special support lent by
his wife. And now the glamorous Diana is a
prized guest at the wealthiest tables – and in the
most bedrooms afterwards . . .

From poverty to nobility, sex siren Diana Saxon
never fails to make the most of her abundant
talent for sensual pleasure!

**FICTION / EROTICA 0 7472 4762 5**

# Bonjour Amour

EROTIC DREAMS OF PARIS IN THE 1950s

*Marie-Claire Villefranche*

Odette Charron is twenty-three years old with enchanting green eyes, few inhibitions and a determination to make it as a big-time fashion model. At present she is distinctly small-time. So a meeting with important fashion-illustrator Laurent Breville represents an opportunity not to be missed.

Unfortunately, Laurent has a fiancée to whom he is tediously faithful. But Odette has the kind of face and figure which can chase such mundane commitments from his mind. For her, Laurent is the first step on the ladder of success and she intends to walk all over him. What's more, he's going to love it . . .

**FICTION / EROTICA 0 7472 4803 6**

Now you can buy any of these other
Delta books from your bookshop or
*direct from the publisher*.

## FREE P&P AND UK DELIVERY
(Overseas and Ireland £3.50 per book)

| | | |
|---|---|---|
| Passion Beach | Carol Anderson | £5.99 |
| Cremorne Gardens | Anonymous | £5.99 |
| Amorous Appetites | Anonymous | £5.99 |
| Saucy Habits | Anonymous | £5.99 |
| Room Service | Felice Ash | £5.99 |
| The Wife-Watcher Letters | Lesley Asquith | £5.99 |
| The Delta Sex-Life Letters | Lesley Asquith | £5.99 |
| More Sex-Life Letters | Lesley Asquith | £5.99 |
| Sin and Mrs Saxon | Lesley Asquith | £5.99 |
| Naked Ambition | Becky Bell | £5.99 |
| Empire of Lust | Valentina Cilescu | £5.99 |
| Playing the Field | Elizabeth Coldwell | £5.99 |
| Dangerous Desires | JJ Duke | £5.99 |
| The Depravities of Marisa Bond | Kitt Gerrard | £5.99 |

## TO ORDER SIMPLY CALL THIS NUMBER

## 01235 400 414

or e-mail orders@bookpoint.co.uk

Prices and availability subject to change without notice.